TRIPLE TEASE

TONY FLOOD

CONTENTS

PRAISE FOR TRIPLE TEASE

Talented former journalist Tony Flood makes an exciting entry into the world of crime writing by treating thriller fans to a triple tease. **PETER JAMES, (number one best-selling crime writer).**

Triple Tease is an addictive thriller that's a real gem! **STUART PINK, THE SUN.**

Do the ends justify the means? That's the moral and ethical sentiment Tony Flood's pacy crime thriller turns on. Super delicious heroine Katrina seeks revenge for the assault on her sister – and gets it! She then challenges compassionate copper DCI Livermore to ignore the rule book and offers to help him trap a serial killer in this sexy, seaside thriller, with the plot twisting and turning right to the climax. There's a nice, detailed sense of place and police procedure here, in a tale brimful with colourful characters – and sensual sex – so hold on tight! If this ever makes it to the screen, DCI Livermore would be a great character to bring to life (with me playing him, of course!). Let's hope Flood gives him another outing – there could be a series in it! **BRIAN CAPRON, actor (serial killer Richard Hillman in 'Coronation Street').**

The clever twists, turns, and thrills kept me glued to the very end. I also loved the frank and vivid sex scenes – it knocks *Fifty Shades of Grey* into the shade! Triple Tease would make a first-class TV thriller, and I can see actors like Stephen Tompkinson queuing up for the lead role of the under pressure, tough yet vulnerable Detective Chief Inspector Livermore. **ALAN BAKER, actor, director, and award-winning writer.**

Triple Tease is a page-turning thriller with plenty of action and explicit sex scenes that keep you wanting more until the very end! A powerful read full of punches and larger-than-life characters! I would recommend Tony Flood's book to anyone who enjoys crime and is looking for a more entertaining and salacious read than the average detective novel. There's brilliant twists that kept me guessing and making sharp intakes of breath more times than I could count. Read it! **EMMY YOSHIDA, author of *CORRUPTED: A Tale of Sex, Scandal & Suspense* and *Community Service.***

Tony Flood writes with the spare authority of his journalistic background and Triple Tease promises enough twists, turns and sex to satisfy thriller readers - **TAMARA MCKINLEY, best**

selling author of Echoes From Afar, and the Beach View Boarding House Series (under the name Ellie Dean).

A good thriller keeps you guessing right until the very end – and *Triple Tease* is a brilliant one. The never-ending twists and turns will have your head spinning as you try to figure out who did what. The enigmatic plot is absolutely fantastic. Every time you think you've got it figured out, something else comes along to leave you baffled. Triple Tease is also wickedly funny, steamily sexy, and impossible to put down. **PATRIC KEARNS, producer-director with Talking Scarlet, actor, and writer.**

Tony Flood has come up with an ingenious, irresistible thriller that really thrills. It's laced with humour and some sizzling sex scenes that, for me, outdo those of E. L. James, Jackie Collins, and Jilly Cooper. They greatly add to a compelling story, with some scenes from a man's viewpoint and others from a woman's to cater for all tastes! **FRANCIS WAIT, author of *Without Their Consent and The Survivalists.***

ALSO BY TONY FLOOD

My Life with the Stars – Best, Ali and the Panties!
  Celebrity book reveals the secrets of Frank Sinatra, Elvis Presley, Joan Collins, George Best, Muhammad Ali, Britt Ekland and a host of other big names interviewed by journalist Tony Flood.

The Secret Potion
  Fantasy adventure, recommended by actress June Whitfield for Harry Potter fans, sees young Jody Richards attempt to rescue her brother, who has been kidnapped by an evil wizard.

Twists in the Tales by The Not Dead Yet Writers,
  featuring two of Tony Flood's short stories
  Sixteen delightful short stories, all with excellent twists in them. There's a mixture of humour, thrills and – in a couple of cases – sexual intrigue.

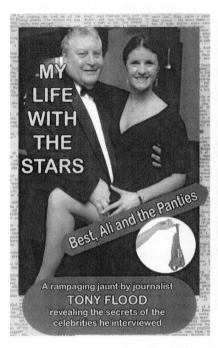

MY
LIFE
WITH
THE
STARS

Best, Ali and the Panties

A rampaging jaunt by journalist
TONY FLOOD
revealing the secrets of the
celebrities he interviewed

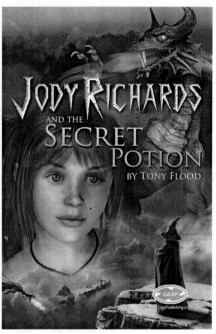

JODY RICHARDS
AND THE
SECRET
POTION
BY TONY FLOOD

TWISTS
IN THE TALES

sixteen superb short stories
A MIXTURE OF HUMOUR, THRILLS AND SEXUAL
INTRIGUE PROVIDE TWISTS GALORE

WE'RE NOT DEAD YET WRITERS

ACKNOWLEDGEMENTS

I owe an enormous debt of gratitude to those 'boys in blue' who have kindly passed on to me so much information about police procedures – and excellent suggestions – based on their vast experience in the force.

By answering my barrage of questions and kindly sharing their knowledge, they have enabled me to add credibility to the storyline in Triple Tease.

I am also extremely grateful to the best-selling author Peter James and his team for their valuable advice and feedback.

As is the case with the information provided by my police contacts, any mistakes that may appear in Triple Tease are mine, not theirs.

Another huge 'thank you' is due to those who have given me further feedback, ideas, and encouragement during the seemingly never-ending re-writing and editing process. They include members of the Anderida Writers group and the creative writing section at Alice Croft House in Eastbourne, as well as crime writer Sheila Bugler, the author of *Hunting Shadows* and *The Waiting Game*.

Two people in particular, who prefer not to be named, have been fantastically supportive.

I am also indebted to the professional, talented and helpful Xlibris publishing team and to those who have provided me with such marvellous endorsements. Thank you all so much!

ABOUT THE AUTHOR

Tony Flood has spent most of his working life as a sports and showbiz journalist.

Tony – formerly controller of information at Sky Television, editor of *Football Monthly* magazine, and sports editor of the Lancashire Evening Telegraph series – retired as a journalist when he left the national Sunday newspaper *The People* in 2010 and has since become a successful author.

His book of celebrity revelations, *My Life with the Stars – Best, Ali and the Panties!*, is packed with stories and anecdotes about the many big names he interviewed from the worlds of show business and sports.

It soared to number one in its category for top 100 e-versions, and features Frank Sinatra, Elvis Presley, Joan Collins, George Best, Muhammad Ali, Linda Gray, Britt Ekland, Frankie Howerd, Patsy Kensit, Petula Clark, Joe Pasquale, Seb Coe, Sir Alex Ferguson, Sir Bobby Charlton, Sir Bobby Robson and many more.

Tony has written books in other genres, including fantasy adventure *The Secret Potion,* recommended by actress June Whitfield for Harry Potter fans. And he is one of nine authors of sixteen intriguing short stories in *Twists in the Tales*. All three of these books have been published by My Voice Publishing.

Tony, who plays football for a Veterans team as a 'goal-hanging' striker trying to reproduce the scoring feats of his youth, also writes theatre reviews for the Brighton Argus and Eastbourne Herald. In addition, he has found time to encourage other authors and writers as chairman of *Anderida Writers* of Eastbourne.

His work as a journalist saw him take on a variety of challenges – learning to dance with Strictly Come Dancing star Erin Boag, becoming a stand-up comedian and playing football with the late George Best and England's World Cup-winning captain, Bobby Moore.

More recently Tony starred on television with former West End actor Alan Baker in 'When Variety was King', which included filmed excerpts from his appearance at the Royal Hippodrome Theatre, Eastbourne, paying tributes to showbiz legends and adding his own brand of humour.

Tony has picked up awards as a journalist and as a writer as well as being honoured in the Eastbourne Resident of the Year awards.

CHAPTER ONE

Wednesday, 17 October 2012

The expression 'drop-dead gorgeous' was never more apt than in the case of Katrina Merton because some men would quite literally die for her.

She was a stunningly attractive twenty-nine-year-old blonde, with a dazzling smile, shapely legs, and fabulous figure – the nearest thing to a younger, taller version of Kylie Minogue.

Katrina was fully aware of the effect she had on the opposite sex, and couldn't resist smiling when noticing a man watching her intently as she walked across the Westerfield College car park in Eastbourne on a dark October evening.

Katrina was heading for a light blue Rover 45 in the right-hand corner of the almost-empty parking area.

The overweight man strode over just before she got to the Rover. "Eh, excuse me," he called. "My evening class has just finished and my car won't start. I was wondering if you could give me a lift to the railway station."

"Can't you just phone a breakdown service?"

"No, I've got to catch a train to get to an appointment. You're my last hope – by the time I realised my car had packed up on me, everyone else had gone."

"Yes, I'm usually one of the last to leave. I'm an art teacher and have to clear up before I go. OK, jump in," she invited, clicking a fob to open the car doors and flashing him a sympathetic smile.

As they both slid into the Rover, her knee-length skirt rode up quite high, revealing a glimpse of her stocking tops. She tugged on the hem but only succeeded in accentuating her full figure in a tight-fitting beige dress.

Suddenly his demeanour changed completely. "Are you a bloody tease?"

"What on earth are you talking about?" Katrina responded, alarmed.

"Forget about the lift, girlie. You and I are going to have sex."

"Are you out of your mind?"

"No, but you must be, parking in the corner of a deserted car park with nobody in sight." As he spoke, he pulled out a flick knife from his pocket and clicked the blade open. "Now, if you don't want me to cut that lovely face of yours, I suggest you do as I tell you."

His icy glare and the menace in his voice were compelling. "You're not the first woman I've 'had' in a car park. And sooner or later, they do what I tell them. You can save yourself a lot of pain by unbuttoning your dress and showing me your tits – do it NOW!"

She met his stare and then started to carry out his instruction. The top two buttons were already undone, and she slowly unfastened two more so that her dress fell open. Beneath was a low-cut white bra with blue trim, which did little to hide a cleavage that would make Dolly Parton proud.

"I've been waiting for you," he said threateningly. "When you came out late last week, I was going to 'have' you then, but someone else was still in the car park. Now you've left yourself a sitting target – a bad mistake, girlie."

He lowered the knife and started to fondle her by pushing one of his huge hands inside the bra and cupping her left breast. Her revulsion was heightened by his foul breath and a trickle of sweat dripping from his double chin.

"You shouldn't have taken so long to put the paints and brushes away," he mocked.

While the creep caressed her nipple, she moved her right hand into an open panel on the driver's side and reached for an object inside it.

"Picture this," he goaded. "You taking off your pretty panties and handing them to me. I love women's panties."

'You're out of luck,' she thought. But Katrina certainly wasn't going to tell this pervert she did not have any on and was wearing the smallest of G-strings! Instead, she replied, "No. You picture this – me shooting you dead."

She was holding a Smith & Wesson snub-nosed revolver in her right hand. "Now get your filthy hands off me, you scumbag. And drop that knife."

She noticed the look of shock on his face which slowly turned to one of defiance, but she held the gun firm, and he finally did as she told him. The knife clattered to the floor.

"You say you've been waiting for me. Well, I've been waiting for you too. One of those women you 'had' was my sister Suzie. It was in this car park three months ago, and it left her traumatised. She's so terrified she still won't go out. That's because you not only sexually assaulted her, but afterwards, you said you'd keep an eye out for her so that you could do it again. You bastard!"

"Oh yeah," he hissed through a puffy pout, which looked as if he'd placed his lips in a wasp's nest. "I remember her. She was a pretty little thing."

"You really are a nasty piece of work. The police haven't been able to do anything, but I knew if I set a trap for you in the same car park, you'd probably try your luck again. Well, now your luck has run out."

"There's nothing you can do, girlie. There's no physical evidence, and it will be just your word against mine. The police won't have a case."

"Who said anything about me involving the police? I'm not going to report you to the police. I'm going to shoot you."

He sniggered. "Oh yeah, and leave blood all over your car?"

"It's not my car. It belongs to one of the students."

"Do you really expect me to believe such a load of nonsense?" he taunted, moving towards her menacingly. "Besides, you haven't got the bottle, so don't waste . . ."

He never finished the sentence. She pulled the trigger and a bullet to the heart killed him instantly.

CHAPTER TWO

Eleven months later:
Tuesday, 3 September 2013

Katrina's sister Suzie, a bewitchingly beautiful brunette, had everything her boyfriend Boris Kimble looked for in a woman – great legs, a well-developed bust, and what he called 'come-to-bed' eyes.

It didn't bother the bigoted solicitor that her IQ would never be as big as her bosoms. Suzie's captivating good looks caused Boris to think about her day and night, but since the sex attack on her last year, she'd refused to give herself completely, and it was driving him mad. If she wasn't such a glamour puss, it wouldn't have been this bad, but she was so desirable he found it hard to keep his hands off her.

Boris watched as she entered the carpeted lounge of her tastefully decorated flat, carefully carrying two glasses of red wine. Was the twenty-year-old iceberg going to unfreeze? Her fully buttoned white linen blouse gave nothing away, but he noticed the black skirt was temptingly short.

Suzie eased herself next to him on the sofa, causing the glasses to wobble. Boris' sexual desires briefly gave way to the fear that she might spill some of the wine on his neatly pressed Gucci grey woollen designer trousers.

He quickly took the glasses and placed them on a small table a few feet away before giving Suzie his undivided attention.

Boris slid closer and kissed her gently on the lips. When she responded, he stroked her elfin-style hair and then her cheek, brushing her only visible facial blemish – a prominent dimple. Eventually, he let his hand drop down to her neck and finally rest on the soft fabric covering two perfectly formed breasts.

He cupped one of them and kissed her again. "You are so lovely, my darling," he muttered as he edged forward, causing her to lean back. More kisses followed.

'*Perhaps I'm about to get an early present,*' mused Boris, who was a few days away from his thirtieth birthday. '*Just take it slowly,*' he told himself, hoping he would finally be rewarded for all the restraint and compassion he'd shown during their relationship in which full sex had been denied him.

'*I must keep the todger under control.*' Unfortunately, he couldn't. It became fully erect and pressed firmly against Suzie's thigh, which was exposed as her skirt rose. The sight of bare flesh and a brief glimpse of pink panties made him more aroused. As a result, his extended member thrust even harder against her leg.

"No!" she yelled in alarm, breaking away from him and pulling her skirt down. "I'm sorry, Boris. I'm not ready for that."

Boris was so frustrated he felt like exploding – verbally if not physically!

"We can't go on like this for much longer, Suzie. You need help," he said as his erection deflated, and he zipped up his trousers.

"You think I should see a therapist?"

"Well, you're certainly sexually dysfunctional," he chided, staring at her through a red mist of suppressed exasperation. "You know how much support and sympathy I've given you since you were attacked by that pervert. But that was over a year ago, and we've never had full intercourse. I have needs, and you're not fulfilling them."

A strand of Boris's wavy blond hair flopped on to his forehead, and he pushed it into place as he stood waiting for his girlfriend to snap back at him. Perhaps he'd gone too far, especially as until recently the trauma she'd suffered had left her afraid to go out.

But instead of coming up with an angry response, she became tearful. Wiping her eyes, she said softly, "It's not because I don't love you, Boris. Actually, I do love you very much."

"And I love you too, Suzie. You mean everything to me."

He took her hands in his and pulled her gently towards him, but he could feel her body become tense. She looked into his eyes and pleaded, "Please give me a little more time."

CHAPTER THREE

Monday, 9 September 2013

When Katrina Merton had received a telephone call, asking her to meet with Detective Chief Inspector Harvey Livermore, she was puzzled almost as much as she was worried. After all, the murder she'd committed in the car park was eleven months ago.

Deciding to dress modestly, Katrina wore a chic grey suit and a high-necked cream blouse. But, with her long blonde locks tumbling over her shoulders, she still looked incredibly sexy.

After being offered a comfortable seat but no tea or coffee by the stern-mannered police chief, Katrina briefly surveyed his colourless office as she waited for him to explain why her presence had been requested on this bleak September morning.

It seemed strange that she'd been summoned from her home in Eastbourne to the high-tech but in decline Sussex House, the specialist crime command in Hollingbury on the fringe of Brighton, to meet a senior officer.

Livermore, a burly man with rugged features and a jutting, bristly chin, didn't take long in providing the answer.

"You will no doubt recall, Miss Merton, that your mother reported a burglary in her home in Newhaven a couple of months back."

"Yes. Does that mean you've caught the thief and recovered my mother's property?"

"It does, indeed. Unfortunately, he'd sold her jewellery, but we've got most of the other items, including your mother's deed box, in which there were bonds and share certificates plus an envelope containing a couple of sensitive documents belonging to yourself. They were passed on to me by the officer dealing with the burglary as they refer to your work in the security service with MI5. I'm now able to return them to you."

He handed her an envelope, which she opened and then glanced at the contents.

"Thank you," she said, giving no explanation.

"I had to check it out and found that you used to process the movements of suspected terrorists and freedom fighters. Fortunately, the thief didn't even look at your papers – they were still in a sealed envelope when we recovered them."

"I'm most grateful, Chief Inspector. As you've seen, the contents concern my work record and a commendation I received. I only worked at a low level, so I don't think keeping them at my mother's would have contravened the Official Secrets Act."

"It's debatable, Miss Merton, because they also refer to techniques and operational duties. I think you should keep them secure or return them to MI5."

"Yes, I will. It would certainly have been embarrassing if these documents had become public knowledge. I greatly appreciate you returning them to me rather than my former employers."

"I used my discretion. May I ask why you stopped working for MI5?"

"I preferred to teach art."

She became aware from his raised eyebrows that he didn't believe this was the real reason, so she elaborated. "I also needed to deal with some personal issues relating to my family life."

"Ah, yes. That would presumably concern the assault on your sister Suzie almost a year ago."

"That's right. It had a devastating effect on her and my mother, so I decided to spend more time with them."

"Hopefully, the fact that the man we believe sexually assaulted your sister, Hugo Protheroe, was later murdered should give her some peace of mind. I had no sympathy at all for him, but there's constant pressure from the press and the chief constable to clear up all murders. That's why we're most interested to find the person who left a set of unidentified fingerprints in the car in which Protheroe was shot. If that person came forward, it would be most helpful."

He stared at her, and in the long silence that followed, she tried unsuccessfully to avoid looking shamefaced. *'Good heavens, he knows they belong to me!'*

"Do you think this is something I can help you with?" asked Katrina, crossing one leg over the other so that the rubbing or nylon against nylon could be heard.

Livermore was briefly distracted and cleared his throat. "I'm simply pointing out that if this person decided to tell us what they were doing in the car, and on what occasion that was, it might eliminate them from our enquiries. Alternatively, they would run the risk that if they were ever arrested, on any matter whatsoever, their fingerprints would automatically be taken and checked against all outstanding marks left at crime scenes. That could put them in a difficult position."

"You already have my fingerprints, Chief Inspector. One of your constables took them, together with those of my mother's and sister's, after the burglary, for elimination purposes. But presumably you're aware of that."

"I am, Miss Merton. Hypothetically, what would you say if your prints matched those in the car in which Protheroe was killed? It was an old Rover 45 parked at Westerfield College where you work as an art teacher."

Katrina's face showed a flash of concern. "Well, it might've belonged to someone at the college who probably gave me a lift at some time."

"Maybe that was the case," conceded the forty-something policeman, again raising his bushy eyebrows in a sceptical manner. "In fact, the Rover had been left in the car park for some weeks by a student, a lad called Landen Patel – he 'dumped it' because the tax and insurance had run out. Was Landen Patel one of your students?"

Before she could answer, Livermore's phone rang. He took the call, and Katrina welcomed the fact she now had time to think, but could not focus. Instead, she felt trapped in this compact, bland office. Katrina noted an absence of any personal pictures or memorabilia, but instead, the policeman's desk was occupied by a computer, an open file, and an in tray that was bulging with papers. More documents had been placed haphazardly on top of a filing cabinet.

'There's hardly room to swing a cat. It's like being in a prison cell – perhaps I soon will be!' Katrina was becoming gripped by fear, and felt her heart pounding.

Her thoughts became scrambled. *'For all my outward display of confidence, I'm riddled with doubt. There are hundreds of insecurities behind my smile. It's almost as if I've got two different personalities . . . I'm constantly challenging myself to face up to life's many problems. It was that fierce determination not to take the easy way out that caused me to confront the rapist in the car park.'*

Katrina suddenly became aware that Livermore had terminated the call, and his grey eyes were dwelling fleetingly on her curvaceous figure before meeting her gaze.

He finally broke the tense silence. "I was asking you if Landen Patel was one of your students."

"Yes, he was. I think he gave me a lift on one occasion. So that's how my fingerprints would be in his car."

"That might explain it," Livermore agreed without conviction in his voice. "However, it doesn't explain the apparent link with Protheroe."

Another uncomfortable silence followed. Katrina's bright blue eyes moved briefly to the window, but the sight that greeted her of the roof of a supermarket opposite did nothing to lift the gloom. Trying to avoid the trap she felt was being set for her, she asked, "Are you certain Protheroe was the man who assaulted Suzie?"

"It's a safe bet. When we discovered his dead body, we checked his DNA with that taken from some of the women who'd previously been attacked and got a perfect match. After your sister was forced to commit a sexual act, she didn't report it until three days later, and we found no DNA evidence, but the manner in which she was assaulted was very similar to some of Protheroe's other victims.

"So the discovery of his dead body in a car containing your prints would be a remarkable coincidence, don't you think? Especially as both crimes occurred in the same car park that you use."

"I suppose so," Katrina acknowledged, trying to remain outwardly calm even though her stomach was tying itself in knots. "But I would've had no way of knowing that it was him who attacked my sister. She still wasn't certain when your colleagues showed her a picture of him."

"Well, she told us how she'd been threatened with a flick knife, and we found such a knife in the Rover 45 alongside the body of Hugo Protheroe. That's another coincidence – and I don't believe in coincidences in murder cases."

Livermore made his right hand into a fist, clenched his other hand around it and pushed until the knuckles cracked.

Katrina found it unnerving. *'Presumably this is a sign of his displeasure.'* She was dreading what he would say next, and her fears were well founded.

"We'll be investigating this matter further, Miss Merton, and I may need to speak to you again."

*****

Katrina was determined to stride out of the police building in a confident manner, but her usual tough persona was crumbling. She was so scared that her legs were in danger of turning to jelly, and she was physically shaking.

This policeman – a chief inspector no less – had discovered that her prints were in the car in which she'd killed that creep Hugo Protheroe. If she was charged with murdering him, then her whole life would be ruined – and her mother and sister would be devastated.

'Don't panic. If you stick to the story that you were given a lift in that car on a previous occasion, the police can't prove anything.'

The trepidation was slowly subsiding. But it was being replaced by the return of the guilt that had consumed her in the months after she shot Protheroe.

Sitting motionless in her parked car, she thought back to that terrible October day when Protheroe fell into her trap. She'd felt she must stop him at all costs because he'd boasted that he would attack her traumatised sister again. But she should've been content to merely threaten the pathetic pervert and give him the fright of his life – killing him had been a huge mistake.

She had to dab her mouth to remove a trace of bile as she recalled how Protheroe's face twisted horrifically when the bullet hit him. And the sight of his dead eyes had haunted her ever since.

Katrina couldn't prevent a tear trickling down her cheek while she bitterly reflected, for the umpteenth time, that she would not have shot him if he hadn't goaded her.

But there was an element of black comedy in it all, she thought. *'What a pity he's not alive to learn that it isn't a good idea to tell a woman with a gun in her hand that she hasn't got the bottle to pull the trigger!*

CHAPTER FOUR

Tuesday, 10 September 2013

"Time's running out," declared Boris. "I've waited long enough. You need to change from being a frightened virgin to a provocative temptress."

"What do you suggest?" she asked, fidgeting on a leather-bound chair in front of him in her dimly lit lounge.

"The problem is, Suzie, that you find it hard to trust any man – even me – following the assault on you, and you apparently can't experience sexual arousal, only fear. Is that right?"

"I suppose it is."

"So I feel you should experiment by being deliberately provocative. If you try to turn me on, you'll hopefully find that it gives you confidence – and pleasure too."

Undeterred by the silence that followed, Boris added, "Shall we give it a go?"

"All right."

"First, I want you to cross your legs seductively so that your skirt rises."

She looked apprehensive but did as he requested, resulting in her short red skirt moving up a couple of inches.

"A little more, please."

She recrossed her long, shapely legs. This time her skirt went higher.

"That's great, Suzie. Seeing a flash of those red suspenders is having a big effect on me already. Eventually, you'll be confident enough to do this in front of other men too."

"I couldn't possibly."

"Don't be so silly. You wouldn't be showing off any more than if you were wearing a swimming costume. It's just that this way it's sexier. Men will be wondering whether you are revealing your suspenders by accident or on purpose – you'll have them begging for more."

"But how will it help ME?"

"You'll know you can arouse men by simply letting them see 'a glimpse of stocking' – it can still be something shocking to misquote the old Cole Porter song. It should give you a great feeling of power, and it will do wonders for your confidence."

"How can you be so sure that just showing men my thighs will arouse them?"

"It's because you're shy and innocent. Your reluctance and uncertainty make you the perfect tease. If some women flashed the flesh, it would have little effect on a man because they'd look cheap and tacky, but others, like you, are real class."

"I find that hard to believe, Boris."

"You want proof? Come over here."

The leggy brunette got up and took four steps forward until she was standing right in front of him.

"Give me your hand." Boris took her left hand and placed it on the bulge at the front of his trousers. "Can you feel how hard I am? You've done that to me simply by flashing your lovely legs. Let me see them again. Lift up your skirt."

She removed her hand from his trousers, stepped back and slowly did as he asked, pulling up the bright red material by the hem to show him the whole of her stocking tops, suspender straps, and silky smooth thighs.

"Higher, my darling – now let me see your panties."

The 'temptress' lifted her skirt further until her small red and white striped bikini briefs were clearly visible.

"What will I see if you move your panties to one side? Will there be hairs or a shaven pussy?"

"I can't talk like that."

"Of course you can. Tell me."

"There's some hairs."

"Show me! Move your panties."

The shapely young woman seemed to freeze.

"Don't be a prick tease, darling."

This had the desired effect. She used her forefinger to pull her briefs to one side, revealing all.

"You naughty girl, Suzie. You've cut your pubic hairs into the cutest little heart. You hussy. And you're wet, aren't you?"

"Sorry. I'm so ashamed," she murmured, turning her head away.

"Don't be ashamed – it's great. Now ask me if I'd like you to take your panties down."

"Must I?"

"Just do it, darling."

"Boris, would you like me to take my panties down?"

"Yes, that would be nice. Please remove your panties."

She slid her briefs slowly to her thighs.

"You look wonderful, Suzie."

"Thank you."

"Now ask if I'd like to touch you between your legs and pleasure you."

"I can't, Boris. Please don't make me do that."

"Nonsense! I want you to say: 'Boris, would you like to play with my pussy?'"

She hesitated again. "Boris, would you . . . would you like to play with my pus . . . pussy?"

"Yes, I would."

Reaching out his left hand, he stroked the heart-shaped hairs and then slid his forefinger along her bud. Confirming it was wet was all the encouragement Boris needed. Her apparently innocent responses were giving him the biggest sexual thrill of his life.

"Look what you've done to me," he cried, taking her hand and pressing it against the front of his trousers. "Pull down the zip and feel inside."

The vision of beauty did as she was bid. She pushed her hand gently inside the open fly and touched the hardness against his pants.

Even in the midst of passion, the fastidious Boris was concerned about his expensive trousers getting creased or soiled. He slipped them off and carefully put them on the chair.

Turning back to her and gazing adoringly at her exposed pussy, he announced, "My cock is rigid. Take it out."

She gently eased her fingers inside the opening of his pants and lifted out his tool.

"Stroke it!"

She did so, rubbing the expanding object gently between the forefinger and thumb of her right hand, until it was fully erect.

"Now you've got a choice – you can either put the cock in your fanny or, better still, you can suck it off."

"I c . . . c . . . can't. Please don't ask me to do that."

His irritation showed as his face reddened with both anger and exertion. She responded by sinking to her knees and using her tongue to good effect.

"Keep licking – that's fantastic . . . Now take it in your mouth – all of it."

Her lips parted, and he thrust the quivering penis between them.

"Pretend it's a lollipop and suck it, darling."

She began to suck tentatively and slowly but, apparently sensing his urgency, quickened the tempo.

Boris increased the sensation even more by pushing her head backwards and forwards, and the effect was so exhilarating he could hardly bear it. But his roughness caused her to resist.

"Sorry! Please don't stop." He stroked her hair gently by way of apology, and she relented. Her tongue pleasured him further, and he groaned in ecstasy. Within seconds his quivering weapon had shot its considerable load.

When he withdrew it from her mouth, she spat out the salty mixture.

"Don't worry – you'll grow to like the taste of it, Suzie," Boris said with a grin, wiping his spent tool.

The woman's demeanour and voice suddenly changed.

"Time to stop the role play, Boris," she rapped. "I don't mind making out I'm this frigid girlfriend of yours, but swallowing a client's cum is something I don't do."

Boris was not offended by the put-down from the sex-for-cash girl named Anna Marie who had impersonated Suzie so well. His head was still reeling from the heights of pleasure he'd experienced.

"Fair enough! You acted out my fantasy perfectly, pretending to be my innocent Suzie." He was so grateful he gave the strumpet an extra £20.

Anna Marie's tone softened as she straightened her bra and popped the note into it, between her pert bosoms. "Thanks very much. It's been a pleasure doing business with you. Most of my clients don't have your imagination. I did find it enjoyable playing a naive, easily shocked virgin being seduced. Even I got turned on at one stage."

Boris was delighted with the compliment the prostitute was paying him. "Anna Marie, you were fantastic," he told her as she opened the door to let him out of her luxury flat. Once in the corridor, he quickly checked to see that his trousers were still immaculately pressed.

CHAPTER FIVE

Wednesday, 11 September 2013

Katrina was still shaken by the apparent discovery of her fingerprints at the scene of the murder but tried to reassure herself that as long as the police couldn't find the gun she'd used, they would have no case against her.

'I must get rid of the blasted thing. I've been stupid to keep it.'

She was reflecting on the situation as she returned to her stylish flat after popping to the newsagents early to buy the *Brighton Argus* and being relieved to find that there was nothing in it for her to be concerned about.

'I mustn't allow myself to get paranoid about this.' Her thoughts were interrupted by the phone ringing. Katrina crossed her lounge to pick it up from the coffee table but didn't make it – her playful kitten Jezebel ran in front of her, tripping her over.

"You silly cat!" she screeched, grabbing hold of the seat of a chair to prevent herself toppling on the floor. A chastised Jezebel ran off into the kitchen. By the time Katrina had recovered, the phone had stopped ringing, but within seconds it sounded again.

It was her sister Suzie wanting to talk about the problems she was having with her boyfriend.

"Boris is upset because I still can't bring myself to have sex with him," Suzie blurted out. "I do love him and obviously find him attractive, but that attack continues to haunt me."

"Well, Boris will just have to wait. He should show more appreciation for your feelings and support you – not put pressure on you," Katrina said, sinking into her big reclining chair after swapping her high heels for comfortable slippers.

"But he's been very supportive and understanding for so long. I feel guilty because I haven't had full sex with him in all the time we've been going together."

"Not even before the attack on you?"

"We used to have the occasional fumble, but I told Boris he'd have to wait until I was ready to go the whole way. Then, after the attack, I couldn't bring myself to even think about having sex. I'm twenty and still a virgin. No wonder Boris is frustrated. He tells me I should see a therapist. What do you think?"

"He might be right, Suzie. It's worth considering. But I thought you'd been getting counselling from a policewoman."

"She's more like a support worker."

"So perhaps a therapist might do you good. They'd not only advise you about your reluctance to have sex, but also about your fears of being attacked again. But, as I've told you repeatedly, you no longer need worry because the creep who attacked you is dead. We both saw his picture in the papers after he was murdered in the car park, didn't we?"

"Yes, it certainly looked like him, though I couldn't be 100 per cent sure. But even if it was him who was killed, there's always the chance of being attacked by another pervert."

Katrina tried to reassure her clearly fragile sister. "It's a danger every woman faces, but you're being so ultra-careful in not going out alone at night that you're minimising the risk. And what happened to that perv Hugo Protheroe should act as a deterrent to any other sickos in our neighbourhood."

"Yes, perhaps my fears are unfounded. If it was Protheroe who attacked me, then he obviously can't carry out his threat to stalk me. You've no idea how awful it was being in that car park after I foolishly agreed to give him a lift . . ."

'Actually, I do,' thought Katrina, recalling her own confrontation with Protheroe.

Suzie was still speaking: ". . . having him paw my body and forcing me to pleasure him was dreadful. But what was just as terrifying was what he said afterwards. I'll never forget him smirking and saying, 'We must do this again, girlie. Don't worry – I'll find you.' I've had so many nightmares about that. Whoever murdered Protheroe did me an enormous good turn. If I ever met them, I'd never be able to thank them enough."

Katrina was tempted to say, "It's me you have to thank, Sis." But she knew Suzie must never find out – if she even suspected, it would cause her more trauma.

CHAPTER SIX

Wednesday, 11 September 2013

Recently promoted Detective Inspector Jeffrey Norris and Detective Constable Grace Conteh were told by Livermore to check if Katrina Merton had ever been given a lift by Landen Patel, the owner of the Rover 45, in which Protheroe had been murdered.

They had traced the former college student to a printing firm where he was a graphic designer, and during his lunch break they took him to a nearby cafe to question him.

Patel, a friendly Indian, chatted freely to them after at first expressing his surprise that the police wanted to speak to him again.

"Your colleagues interviewed me at the college when that guy was found murdered in my car, and I told them all I knew," he said. "I had no idea what he was doing in the car."

"Further information has come to light, and we need to check a few more details with you," explained DI Norris.

"OK, fire away."

"Were you one of Katrina Merton's pupils?" asked the policeman, taking off his glasses and wiping the lenses which had become clouded by the steam wafting from his coffee.

"Yes. Miss Merton taught me art and graphic design for about twelve months."

"During that time, did you ever give her a lift in your car?"

"Not that I can recall."

"Are you quite sure about that?" Norris persisted, putting his spectacles on again so that he could make a note of what the youngster was telling him.

"I can't swear to it, man, but it's something I think I would have remembered. Katrina Merton is one fit lady, and giving her a ride in my car would surely have stuck in my memory. There was one occasion when about six people crammed into the old jalopy after a party, but I don't remember Miss Merton being one of them."

"Did she ever ask to borrow your car?"

"No."

"Who else drove it apart from you?"

"My mate Jezza did on a couple of occasions. That was during the first few months I was at the college, but after that I stopped using the car when the tax and insurance ran out. I just left it in the college car park."

"Did anyone borrow it after that?"

Patel hesitated and stroked his goatee as if contemplating.

"There's no need to worry," the inspector assured him. "I'm not going to 'do' you or your mates for driving without tax or insurance. But it's important we know if someone else used it."

"Well," replied Patel at length, "when I stopped driving I left the car keys in my locker. I did say that any of the other students were welcome to use it if they paid to get it taxed or insured. Nobody took me up on the offer."

"But they could have driven the car without getting it taxed or insured," suggested DC Conteh, a pretty Jamaican. Her broad smile seemed to disarm the young man.

"I suppose they might have done outside college hours. I'd have been none the wiser if they'd taken the keys from my locker and then put them back."

"But wouldn't they have found it difficult to get into your locker?" Norris queried.

"Not really – the lock was a bit dodgy."

Norris had another question. "Did Miss Merton know about your car keys being in your locker?"

"Probably – it was pretty common knowledge."

*****

"Have you ever come across Katrina Merton, Grace?" Nottage asked after Patel had gone back to work.

"No, but her sister Suzie's been receiving support from my friend WPC Hazel Maxwell, who's responsible for the welfare of rape victims. Hazel happened to mention to me that Suzie was so traumatised, following the attack on her in the

ld College car park, she was scared to go out for
erwards. And she was worried sick that Katrina had
put herself at risk by working as an art teacher at the college."

Nottage took off his glasses and blinked like a meerkat while wiping the lenses again.

"Surely her worries should have been over following the murder of that rapist in the same car park. Hell, that's a bit of a coincidence, isn't it? – Katrina working at the very place where her sister was sexually assaulted and the rapist was murdered?"

His colleague looked up from munching on her vegetarian sandwich. "Yes, but surely that's all it is."

"Possibly. If I remember correctly, all the fingerprints taken from the front of that Rover have been identified apart from one set, which look like a woman's. Now, if that set belonged to Katrina or Suzie, the question is: was one of them merely in the car as a passenger at some time, or could she have been the driver who killed Protheroe?"

*****

As they got up to leave, a tall, smartly dressed young man bustled past like a human whirlwind and almost knocked Conteh off balance.

"Sorry," he called over his shoulder, continuing to move swiftly towards the exit. Then suddenly he stopped, swivelled around, and called, "It's Grace, isn't it? Grace Conteh."

"Yes," Conteh confirmed, turning to face him. He looked familiar, but she couldn't place him.

"I'm Ross Yardley. We went to grammar school together. My, you've changed! I almost didn't recognise you."

"Likewise. Mind you, it was sometime ago, and we were only fifteen."

"It's great to see you," Yardley gushed, his handsome features creasing into a big grin. "What are you doing now?"

"I'm working for the police force as a detective constable, and this is my colleague DI Nottage."

Yardley and Nottage exchanged the briefest of nods.

"And you?" asked Conteh.

"I'm a freelance journalist. Look, I've just taken a call, asking me to do a job, so I'm in a rush. Why don't we meet up to chat about old times? How about a drink at the Lion pub in The Lanes tomorrow evening?"

"OK, Ross, you're on. Let's make it 6.30."

As Yardley disappeared, Conteh noticed that Nottage was peering at her oddly. It seemed to be a look of disapproval. Then it struck her. *'Have I made a big mistake in agreeing to go out with a journalist?'*

CHAPTER SEVEN

Wednesday, 11 September 2013

An agitated Katrina paced her flat in a haze after receiving a message on her answerphone from one of her former students.

She played it a second time. "Hi, Miss Merton. It's Landen Patel. I thought you should know that the police have been asking me if I ever gave you a lift in my Rover in which that guy was shot. I told them I couldn't remember doing so, but they seem to think you've been in the car."

"Bloody hell!" she cursed. "They obviously suspect me of killing Protheroe. And if they arrest me, it will leave my sister and mother devastated again. If only there was something I could do about it."

Then she remembered the article she'd read in the previous day's paper about DCI Livermore getting nowhere with the investigation into the killing of two women. She eventually managed to find where she'd discarded the paper and reread the story.

The writer, Ross Yardley, was critical of the police. He pointed out that Livermore had arrested a man for the murders but released him due to insufficient evidence, and there was concern that the killer would strike again.

Yardley went on to criticise the police chief for finding the time to give a talk at a WI meeting.

Turning on her laptop, Katrina looked up details about the local WI and their meeting at which Livermore was due to talk. It was tonight.

She suddenly had a brainwave. *'Perhaps there is something I can do.'*

*****

Katrina sat at the back of the community centre hall listening to DCI Livermore's interesting talk to about forty WI members on what precautions women could take to reduce the risk of being victims of crime.

'That newspaper reporter missed the point completely,' she thought. *'Far from wasting his time, Livermore is passing on valuable advice and giving the WI members reassurance.'*

She did not make her presence known until the policeman was about to leave. Then, barging her way in front of a huge woman, who was about to attach herself to him, Katrina walked alongside Livermore and asked if she could have a few words.

"What can I do for you, Miss Merton?" he replied brusquely as they walked out of the building.

"Actually, I think there's something I can do for you, Chief Inspector."

"This is rather inappropriate, Miss Merton, especially as I'm intending to invite you back to Sussex House to interview you under caution regarding the murder of Hugo Protheroe."

She blanched but refused to be put off. "Perhaps you might want to take a rain check on that when you realise what I have in mind."

"If it's what I think it is, then you'll be wasting your time, Miss Merton."

"You've got it wrong, Chief Inspector. What I'm offering is not my body but my help in catching the serial killer who's so far eluded you and caused you to be heavily criticised in the press."

They were now walking along the road together.

"And what are you suggesting?"

"I've read up on the murders of two local women and see that both of them were members of a dating agency in Brighton. You arrested a male member of the same agency but had to let him go through lack of evidence. Well, if I joined that dating agency, I could make a point of going out with your main suspect and helping you catch him."

"I think you've been watching too many far-fetched television programmes, Miss Merton."

"You seem to forget that I worked for MI5, so I'm not naive about undercover operations. I processed reports from surveillance teams who followed the movements of terrorists and tapped their phone calls. I would be the perfect person to help you carry out such an operation."

"And just why would you make me this offer?"

"I think you know."

They had reached Livermore's car. He opened the passenger door and invited her to get in.

When they were both seated, he stared at her. Katrina felt obliged to speak again. "You say you were planning to interview me under caution – presumably about my fingerprints being in the Rover. I thought I'd explained that to you. I was given a lift in the car at some time – if not by Landen Patel, then by one of his friends."

"You don't sound too sure. I think this particular topic is something we should discuss at the police station."

"Can't we talk informally about it now? Loads of students were probably passengers in that car at one time or another – sometimes spaced out after a few drinks. I don't see why it's so difficult for you to accept that I was among them."

"Perhaps you drove the car yourself?"

"No, I didn't."

"But you knew that Patel kept the keys in his locker."

"So did a lot of people – that's just circumstantial."

"No doubt you would claim it was only circumstantial that you used the same college car park in which Hugo Protheroe was murdered. The same car park where we believe he sexually assaulted your sister three months earlier."

"So what are you suggesting, Chief Inspector?"

"I'm suggesting that you had a good motive to kill him."

"Yes, I had a motive, but, no doubt, so did many other women if he was a rapist."

"Unlike them, you were working in the college, holding an evening class on the night of the murder."

"So are you planning to arrest me?" Katrina's attempt at posing the question as a challenge did not work because she was trembling with fear.

Livermore didn't answer, so she continued. "I'm hoping that your concerns about me and the Rover can become academic if I help you by catching another pervert."

"Ah, yes. The plan you mentioned just now for you to meet our murder suspect through his dating agency and get him to confess."

Katrina sighed, causing Livermore's smirk to change to a smile. It gave her some encouragement.

"I think you need to take my offer seriously, Chief Inspector. You believe this killer could strike again, don't you? And I could help you prevent it by acting as bait. If he attacks me while you're keeping surveillance, then other women will no longer be in danger."

"What you're proposing is unethical, Miss Merton, and completely against police procedures. I am duty-bound to follow them."

"You mean the way they were followed while the Yorkshire Ripper killed thirteen women? And when all those poor kids were sexually assaulted while Jimmy Savile and Cyril Smith escaped prosecution? Yes, you'd be breaking the rules – but you could be saving a woman's life. I think you should seriously consider what I'm offering you."

CHAPTER EIGHT

Thursday, 12 September 2013

Katrina was mad at herself. *'How stupid of me making such a damn-fool proposal to a senior police officer! All I've done is to convince him that I killed Protheroe.'*

She was certain she'd be seeing Livermore again soon and would have to answer his questions under caution at the nick. It turned out she was half-right.

Instead of being summoned to go back to his office, Katrina received a shock visit from him.

"Do come in, Chief Inspector," she greeted, showing him into the trendy living room of her flat in a secluded road in Rottingdean. "If you wanted to see me again so soon, you should've invited me out on a date."

"Unfortunately, this is strictly business, Miss Merton."

'Flirting with this man isn't going to work', Katrina decided. She could see that the low-cut top she was wearing was having little effect on him, though his gaze did flicker briefly over her

cleavage. At least she could try to appeal to his 'softer' side. "Please call me Katrina."

The policeman cleared his throat. "Very well, Katrina."

"Do have a seat. Have you come to discuss my proposal?"

He chose to sit on an upright chair rather than join her on the studio couch. "As I told you last night, your suggestion would be in complete contravention of police procedures."

"But following police procedures has failed to catch the killer. The rule book prevents you from using one of your pretty young policewomen as the bait in a honeytrap, but you can use me."

Livermore leaned back in his chair and smiled at her. "Normally I would never entertain your idea in a million years. But you're right about one thing – I'm worried the killer will strike again before I can get enough evidence to put him away.

"You say you've read in the papers that a man was arrested and taken into custody three months ago concerning the sexual assaults and murders of two women. His name is Justin Remington, and he met them both through a Brighton dating agency. But we were unable to take the case to court due to a . . . technicality." He shook his head before continuing. "Remington should be behind bars – unfortunately, he's not. He's now out on the streets again, and free to resume his membership with the dating agency. In fact, he already has, which means that other women are at risk."

"So do you agree that I could help you catch him?"

"I can't stop you joining the dating agency if you choose to do so, and should you subsequently tell me that you are concerned about your safety, I'd protect you. You'd certainly be a likely target. The two victims who were stabbed to death were very similar to you. Both were good-looking blondes in their late twenties or early thirties, and were professional, single women. It would seem you're Remington's ideal type. If he saw your picture on the agency's website, he'd almost certainly want to meet you."

"And if he made an attempt to rape me, then I could give evidence against him in court."

Livermore shook his head once more. "It's unlikely to be that easy, Katrina."

"I'm aware of that, Chief Inspector. My work with MI5 taught me this sort of thing can be a long process. But I'm prepared to go out on a few dates with him if necessary – providing you keep us under surveillance."

"And what would you want in return? Presumably, if you helped me nick Remington, you'd expect me to accept your explanation that the reason your prints were in the Rover was because you'd once taken part in a joyride. I should stress that I don't advocate anyone taking the law into their own hands and committing a revenge killing, even on a serial rapist like Protheroe."

Katrina weighed up her options. "Can I talk to you completely off the record?"

"Go ahead."

"I'm not offering to go out with this suspect of yours because I see myself as some sort of vigilante. If I'd killed Protheroe, it would have given me no pleasure – I haven't got a bloodlust. His victims – including my sister – might believe that we're well rid of him, but shooting him would be something I'd be ashamed of doing.

"And if I was charged with murder – or even manslaughter – it would leave my mother and sister completely shattered. That's why I'm proposing a deal. So the big question, Chief Inspector, is, can I trust you?"

Livermore smiled again. "It's more a case of whether I can trust you, Katrina. Even if I accept what you say about not being a cold-blooded killer, I'd have to put one hell of a lot of faith in you to carry out your audacious scheme. If it came to light, I'd be thrown out of the force. Then another officer would be put in charge. So there can be no guarantees."

"What do you mean exactly?"

"Let's say you help me catch Remington and I don't investigate further what your prints were doing in the Rover. That means I wouldn't be ordering a search of your flat or car – or questioning you or your relatives. But should another officer become aware you'd been in the Rover, they'd want confirmation it wasn't at the time of Protheroe's murder. If that confirmation couldn't be provided, then you may be arrested. So there's still a risk."

"That's fair enough," she assured him. "It's a chance I'm willing to take – are you?"

"OK. But if it wasn't for your exemplary record with MI5, I wouldn't be giving you this opportunity. You do understand that this meeting we're having now has never taken place?"

"My lips are sealed. So our only contact has been in your office when you returned my documents."

"We'd also have to admit to bumping into each other at the WI meeting because people saw us there last night. But we've never discussed Remington. You simply decide to join a dating agency and just happen to meet him. Should he attack you, the only way we'd get a conviction would be if this arrangement is never revealed."

"Are you sure he's still a member of the same agency? I'd have thought they would have removed him from their books."

"Yes, he's still with them. In the course of our murder investigations, we interviewed all their male clients, so presumably the agency felt that as Remington and the others were not charged they must be innocent."

"What happens if our honeytrap works and I have to give evidence against him?"

"You'd simply tell the truth about your dates with Remington and what occurs."

Katrina nodded in agreement. "I won't let you down, Chief Inspector. But if it turns out that Remington is not the killer, I'm going to feel guilty about stringing him along."

"I'm as sure as I can be that he's the murderer. As you've said yourself, Katrina, our justification for doing this is to ensure that he doesn't kill again."

Livermore got to his feet. "Your safety will be my number one priority. If Remington threatens you in any way, an undercover man will immediately come to your rescue. I'll let you know the details later. Is that all clear and acceptable?"

"Perfectly clear."

"And acceptable?"

"Yes. I won't let you down."

Once Livermore had told her how to contact him and then departed, Katrina was in a far better frame of mind. *'I'll no longer be faced with the problem of having to dispose of the gun in a hurry. But I could be putting my life at risk.'*

CHAPTER NINE

Thursday, 12 September 2013

His resentment had turned to anger at an early age and become worse in his teenage years when his sexual desires were not fulfilled.

At school he was a loner. When he did try to hang around with the boys in his class, he was consumed with envy as they boasted of touching up girls behind the cycle sheds. His own clumsy attempt to try it on with a busty blonde called Vicky ended in her pushing him away and telling him he was disgusting.

As he grew older, he lusted after women, but his lack of finesse resulted in more rejections. And buying every girly magazine he could afford to help him regularly indulge in masturbation still left him deeply frustrated.

The voices in his head – 'the demons' he called them – told him that women were bitches who delighted in humiliating him. Yet he continued to pursue them. He turned his attentions to the plain Janes, and one even threw herself at him!

She was a plump spinster who ironically was called Jane. But it was not only in the looks department that Jane was deficient; she would either giggle as if she was a silly schoolgirl or stare at him like a lovesick sow. Grateful for small mercies, he took advantage of her infatuation for him by rogering her from behind. This meant he didn't have to look at her chubby face dripping with beads of sweat that turned her running mascara into a messy swamp.

He tried to fantasise he was having it away with one of the world's most glamorous sex symbols, but Jane usually shattered that illusion by either burping or farting. The upshot was that he only came twice in seven increasingly frantic attempts!

"I'm scoring less often than the bloody England football team in a World Cup tournament!" he chastised himself. So he swiftly brought the relationship with Jane to an end.

CHAPTER TEN

Thursday, 12 September 2013

The Lion public house, right in the middle of The Lanes, a collection of narrow Brighton alleyways famous for their antique and jewellery shops, had a cavern-like feel.

It was a popular, lively pub with a warm atmosphere, but Grace Conteh was now cursing Ross Yardley's choice of venue for their early evening meeting because it meant her driving into town after a hectic Thursday grind.

Even though she'd spent very little time reapplying her make-up and combing through her short, black curly hair, she was running late. It took ages to get through a traffic jam, and by the time she'd found somewhere to park her clapped-out old Honda, she arrived almost twenty minutes later than agreed.

After pushing her way through the crowded bar, Grace found Ross gazing at photographs by local artists on one of the walls.

"Hi," he said. "I was beginning to fear you'd forgotten we had a date." It was the mildest of rebukes, and Grace noted that the sight of her dressed smartly in black, with the exception of a white blouse, brought a smile to his face. She was immediately aware that, although she was not a natural beauty, this man was attracted to her.

Ross bought her a Martini and lemonade and they managed to find seats on a comfortable sofa, which another couple had just vacated.

"How long have you been in the police force?" he asked her.

"About five years. I started on the beat and now work in CID. I love it."

"And what had you been doing when I bumped into you?"

"Oh, DI Nottage and I had just been making a routine check," Grace answered, non-committally. "How did your story work out?"

"Fine. I got some great quotes from an old guy who's getting married on his ninety-eighth birthday," he replied, flashing his infectious grin. "I do general news as a freelance and have written for most of the national tabloids. You may've seen my byline."

"Yes," Grace lied. "I probably have, but if I saw your name I didn't realise the connection."

As she spoke, Grace noticed that her companion was pushing something into his mouth and chewing it.

"You wouldn't be satisfying a drug habit in front of a police officer, would you, Ross?"

"Actually, I'm kicking a habit, but not in the way you mean. It's only gum I've got in my mouth. I gave up cigarettes last month, and chewing gum helps me to take my mind off a craving for nicotine."

Grace's look of disapproval gave way to a broad smile.

They then talked about their schooldays, each trying to remember the names of old classmates and teachers.

Grace was enjoying herself in the company of this good-looking, attentive man, with bright blue eyes and well-groomed fair hair. But she was on her guard. *'I'd better not tell him I had a crush on him at school and now find him even more attractive.'*

Big alarm bells sounded in her head when Ross brought the subject back to her work. *'I mustn't let anything slip about the case I'm involved with. Is he simply making conversation or trying to pump me for information to use in the papers?'*

The evasive police constable was relieved she could use the excuse that she found it hard to hear some of what Ross was saying because of the music being played by an exuberant DJ.

A mix of Motown, funk, mod revival and punk rock was uplifting. Grace even swayed on her seat to the ska sound combining elements of Caribbean calypso with American jazz and rhythm and blues.

She was pleased when Ross suggested a second date in a quiet upmarket restaurant. She liked his clean-cut imagine, smooth features, and mischievous grin so she readily agreed.

Only after she'd accepted the invitation did Grace think about the possible consequences. *'What would my colleagues feel about me dating a journalist during an ongoing murder investigation?'* But her heart was ruling her head.

CHAPTER ELEVEN

Monday, 16 September 2013 to Wednesday, 25 September 2013

Katrina wasted no time in making an appointment for herself at the plush Brighton office of Dream Dates and Friendships Incorporated with 'chief matchmaker' Melissa Frothington-Smythe.

Melissa was as posh as her double-barrelled surname inferred and spoke in a genteel voice while repeatedly referring to the fact that she ran an exclusive upmarket introduction service.

When Melissa turned in her high-backed swivel chair to type in her new client's details on a computer, her heavily made-up features were no longer visible. In fact, Katrina could only see the woman's right hand.

"So," Melissa probed, "are you looking for someone with whom you can have a casual social relationship or a potential marriage partner?"

"I'm completely open-minded about it," said Katrina, addressing the hand. "It will depend entirely on what the gentlemen in question are like."

Melissa entered another answer before turning around to face her new member. "I've put down 'optional'. That completes our questionnaire, so it just remains for you to pay our £500 joining fee and then our monthly subscription of £90."

'That's steep. I don't suppose DCI Livermore is going to reimburse me,' thought Katrina.

Melissa continued her spiel. "We're not the cheapest dating agency but definitely one of the best, specialising in single professional clients. We're discreet and selective."

Katrina had already seen Dream Dates' website containing pictures of fanciable women next to handsome well-dressed men, plus testimonials from satisfied clients ranging from company directors and financial advisers to teachers and solicitors.

"Presumably not all your clients are as good-looking as those on your website, are they? But looks aren't everything."

"Quite so."

"Do you run checks on your clients?"

"We do – extensively. But we always act with the utmost discretion."

After accepting the membership fee, Melissa explained for the second time how she would match Katrina with those male clients whose details suggested they were most suitable for her, and then offer her a date with one of them.

Within two days Katrina received details of a gentleman called Ted Blessington, a tall, pleasant-looking waterboard inspector. She went out to dinner with him but found him boring and not at all her type.

She explained this to Melissa and was 'matched' with the owner of a bathroom showroom who proved equally unappealing when they met for a lunchtime chat. He was in good shape physically, but his main topics of conversation were his interests in trains and stamps – and how many toilet suites he'd sold that month!

This time Katrina stressed to Melissa that she needed to be paired with someone who was more exciting – and that looks didn't matter to her. She was provided with pictures of three other clients, one of whom she could tell, from police photos shown to her previously, was Justin Remington. Dream Dates and Friendships were still promoting him as one of their 'five star' clients despite the fact he had gone out with two murdered women and was the number one police suspect. So much for Melissa's 'extensive checks'!

Katrina was given Justin's phone number, but she was nervous about ringing him. She sat for several minutes staring at the telephone in her hand before finally plucking up the courage to take this possibly dangerous step.

It was reassuring that Remington sounded anything but a pervert. He was charming and polite and told Katrina his job as a financial adviser involved him dealing with several leading companies.

They chatted for some time, and when Katrina mentioned she loved Italian food, he took the bait.

"How would you like to come out to dinner with me?" he asked.

"That would be nice. I'm free on Friday evening."

"So am I. Let's make it Friday then. I'll take you to an Italian restaurant where the food and atmosphere are awesome."

The only downside was that the exotic eatery was near to where he lived in Seaford, and Katrina would be out of her comfort zone.

CHAPTER TWELVE

Wednesday, 25 September 2013

As soon as Livermore received details from Katrina about her date with Remington, he invited his old mate and golf partner 'Buster' Bates for a lunchtime drink.

Bates had been a shining light in the police force as a highly rated detective sergeant until he was sacked for being convicted of drink-driving while on holiday in Cornwall.

The thin but muscular cockney now worked for a retail bank, investigating credit card fraud.

"So," he said, sipping a pint of lemonade and lime in the corner of the saloon bar of the Sailor's Retreat. "Is this just a social get-together, or have you got something in mind?"

"I want you to do me a favour."

"What, another one? What's it this time?"

"Do this for me and we'll call it all square after me helping you land the cushy job that's bringing you in more dosh than you ever dreamed of earning as a copper."

"Just what have you got in mind?"

"This should be like old times for you, Buster. After all, you were trained in surveillance, weren't you? I want you to help me keep an eye on Justin Remington, starting this Friday."

Buster, having just taken another mouthful of his soft drink, almost spat it out. "Bloody hell, Harvey! Don't you ever give up? Remington is the bloke you arrested for two murders, but couldn't get the CPS to take to court, isn't he?"

"One and the same, Buster."

"I thought you already had him under surveillance."

"We did until the Chief pulled the plug. He said it wasn't getting us anywhere because Remington hadn't put a foot wrong for over two months – and deploying up to twenty officers was eating away our budget. But now I've learned that Remington is going on a date with a stunning blonde who looks very much like those two murdered women."

"Harvey, be reasonable, mate. I can't spend my days watching him when I've got my own job to do."

"I am being reasonable, Buster. This shouldn't interfere with your work. All I want you to do initially is help me keep Remington under surveillance on two or three evenings while he's with this young lady. I can't leave her without protection, but neither can I afford to get my officers to provide it because, if I do, I'll finish up like you – thrown out of the force."

"How come?"

"Firstly, because my boss would never authorise further surveillance without solid evidence, which I haven't got. And secondly, because the blonde, who is the eye candy in what amounts to a honeytrap, is a civilian."

"Have you lost your marbles, Harvey? You could be jeopardising your whole career, man. Why take such a crazy risk?"

"I'm convinced Remington has killed twice and will do so again unless I stop him."

Buster shook his head, and his craggy face creased into a grin. "I get that, Harvey, but I've a feeling there's even more to it. Am I right?"

It was obvious that Buster would not be fobbed off without some further explanation, so he gave him one.

"If you must know, the mother of one of the victims inadvertently contaminated the forensics evidence on Remington by touching things in the flat in which she found her daughter's body. You can imagine how devastated the poor woman was at discovering her daughter dead. To then learn that she may have messed up our chances of convicting the murderer was a crushing blow. I promised I'd bring her justice, and I mean to keep my word."

Buster held up his large hands in mock surrender. "Fair enough. But it's bizarre that you, one of the straightest coppers in the force, have suddenly turned into a maverick. So, what's the plan?"

"This blonde is going out to dinner with Remington tomorrow night. I want you to be in your car nearby, listening in on a bugging device hidden in a mobile phone I'm giving her. If she mentions the code word 'sneeze', then you spring to her rescue."

"And you think it will be that simple?" Buster scoffed.

"No, of course, it won't. That's exactly what I said to the young lady who is assisting me in this undercover operation. Remington is unlikely to make a move on her until he gets her alone, and that might not happen on a first date. But if we keep watch for two or three dates, I'm pretty sure he'll threaten her at some stage."

"And you're prepared to risk that with just a one-man surveillance team?"

"The alternative is for me to do nothing while Remington goes out with other women from the dating agency he's using – and those women will have no protection at all. If our girl needs assistance, then you come running. You won't be acting completely alone – I'll be on hand to back you up if necessary."

"Just who's this mystery woman? And why is she agreeing to put herself at risk by helping you, Harvey?"

"Her name is Katrina Merton, and she was formerly with MI5. She's the sister of a girl who was attacked by a rapist called Hugo Protheroe."

"Protheroe? He's the guy who was shot in a car park, isn't he?"

"That's right."

"So this Katrina is on a crusade to get rapists off our streets, is she?"

"Something like that, Buster. She's ideal for this task because she knows about surveillance from working with MI5. But I need you to act as her protector."

His friend did not appear to be completely won over.

"Just supposing, Remington takes the bait, attacks Katrina, and I nab him. How do you think this will play out in court, Harvey? The defence will claim agent provocateur."

"That's why I've chosen you, Buster, my old son. If we catch him, you'll claim that you just happened to be passing nearby, heard Katrina scream, and came rushing to her rescue. You'll be a hero – and Remington will be caught bang to rights."

CHAPTER THIRTEEN

Thursday, 26 September 2013

Livermore's next port of call was Katrina's flat in Rottingdean where he explained her role and issued her with a mobile phone, into which had been placed a very small ultra-high frequency bugging device.

"When you meet up with Remington tomorrow, make sure you have this mobile in your coat or bag next to you," the policeman told her. "Then my surveillance man can hear your conversation, and you'll be able to summon help if necessary. You'll be quite safe inside the restaurant, but it's vital we monitor you when you're alone with Remington. He'll probably walk you to your car afterwards and may ask you to give him a lift, so that's when you could be at risk."

Livermore also gave her a coded phrase. "If you feel in any danger at all, just say the words 'Sorry, I think I'm going to sneeze'. My man Buster and I will be listening to receivers in unmarked cars nearby. Once we hear you say the word 'sneeze', Buster will come running immediately."

Katrina looked sceptical. "But if Remington decides to knife me, then he'll probably do it before the cavalry arrives."

"Don't worry," the DCI assured her. "Based on the murderer's profile, he's more likely to persuade you to invite him into your flat and make his move there. But we won't take any chances. If you give him a lift and he tries anything in your car, you should still have plenty of time to tip us off. My man will be very close at hand and will rush to your aid immediately."

Katrina put the mobile in her bag. "Does it work as a phone as well as a bugging device?"

"Yes. I've put a number on it for you to use if you want to talk to me at any time. I've got myself a spare pay-as-you-go mobile, which only you can access. So don't phone me on the office line – just on this number. And don't use this mobile to phone anyone else."

"How do you think I should act with Remington? Should I flirt with him or be stand-offish?"

"Just act normal at first. But if he doesn't 'come on' to you, then I suggest you tease him a little."

"Tease him?" she repeated in a questioning tone, staring into Livermore's grey eyes as they sat opposite each other in her lounge.

"Yes, you should let Remington see a few glimpses of your considerable assets, but only allow him to look – not touch. If you were to submit, there would be no reason for him to threaten you, would there?"

"I understand. I'll give him the triple tease."

It was the policeman's turn to repeat what was said as a question. "The triple tease?"

"Yes. I'll show him teeth, thighs and . . ."

"Tits," he finished for her.

Katrina nodded, pleased that the somewhat-dour police chief was at last responding to her impish sense of humour. "I think a big smile plus a glimpse of my thighs and cleavage should do the trick." She crossed her legs provocatively as she spoke.

"Yes," replied the normally unruffled Livermore, appearing to show signs of embarrassment. "I didn't think I'd need to spell out to you how you should act."

"What do you mean, Chief Inspector?" she asked in mock indignation.

"We both know that most women are capable of arousing men quite easily. The lady who was in that Rover with Hugo Protheroe might have done so unintentionally before he pulled a knife on her and she shot him. On the other hand, she may have been setting a trap for him by teasing him."

She felt like saying "He didn't need much teasing", but limited herself to a shake of the head and a barely audible "Bullshit!"

CHAPTER FOURTEEN

Friday, 27 September 2013

At least the brief sexual relationship with the buxom spinster called Jane had made him more confident.

He found that when the anger – and the voices – did not invade his thoughts, he could engage with women reasonably well. And his problems seemed to be over when Rochelle, a tall, well-groomed divorcee, came into his life. He was delighted to discover that she shared his love of rough sex, and within weeks she had moved in with him.

She brought out the best in him, and he was able to banish the dark side of his 'Jekyll and Hyde' split personality while he was with her.

But her non-stop shopping sprees made him realise that what mainly attracted her to him was his money. Confirmation of this came when she took most of what was left of it and walked out on him. 'Mr Hyde' promptly returned!

His lustful cravings became worse, and his frustrations increased with the awareness that most women were unlikely to willingly submit to how far he wanted to go with them.

As he slid further into his hate-filled demonic world, rejection was something he could no longer tolerate.

Two women had tried to say 'no' to him, but they wouldn't do it again – they were no longer alive!

CHAPTER FIFTEEN

Friday, 27 September 2013

Katrina took a lot of time choosing what to wear for her date with Justin. How appealing did she want to look to a suspected rapist and murderer? Her jangling nerves added to her dilemma before she finally settled for a stylish woollen red dress with a buttoned front and a hem that finished just above the knee. She left the top two buttons unfastened.

As she applied her coral-red lipstick, her hand began to shake. *'Come on, Katrina,'* she scolded herself. *'You can do this.'* With that, she brazenly undid another button.

She knew from the picture of Justin on the dating agency website that he wouldn't look anywhere near as good as he'd sounded on the phone, but he would almost certainly be well dressed. She was right. Justin, wearing a smart sports jacket, appeared older than his thirty-two years, with lines under his narrow brown eyes, and slightly receding hair.

A Campari and orange before they ordered their meal helped to settle her uneasiness, and as they chatted, she was pleased to find that Justin was proving a charming companion.

This confident man had the gift of the gab. He talked at length about a variety of subjects, which he made sound interesting, including his love of the theatre, and Katrina had to admit to herself that he was quite fascinating. *'He seems nothing like a killer.'*

The food and wine in the trendy little Italian restaurant in which they were dining were a delight, so what had promised to be a date from hell was actually proving quite enjoyable.

The fact that Justin didn't gawp at her cleavage or her legs like so many men did helped her to relax – until she suddenly became aware of something she'd overlooked.

'Oh damn! The bug . . . I've left the mobile phone in the pocket of my coat, and the waitress has hung it up.'

"Excuse me, Justin," she spluttered. "I just need to visit the ladies' room." With that, she went to the cloakroom, retrieved the mobile and put it in her handbag."

On returning, Katrina placed her handbag next to her. *'I hope I don't look guilty. Have I aroused his suspicions?'*

She gave him her broadest smile and received one back. But whereas his was more like a bashful grin, hers had the radiance of a model in a toothpaste advertisement.

"You said on the phone that you're something of a financial expert . . ."

"I'm supposed to be. Yes, I'm a financial adviser for my sins."

"Have you done that kind of work long?" Katrina asked, even though she already knew the answer, having gleaned everything she could about him from DCI Livermore and the biography given to her by Melissa Frothington-Smythe.

"About five years. It's well paid but not very exciting. I work mainly for companies, giving them financial projections, though I do have a few private clients as well. But I won't go into detail – it would all sound very boring."

"Nowhere near as boring as the guy I went out with whose only interests were trains and stamp collecting," she assured him. "Oh, I hope I haven't put my foot in it. You're not into trains and stamps, are you?"

"No, I'm not quite that boring. Tell me about yourself. You're a teacher, aren't you?"

"Yes. I give short courses on art and design at Westerfield College. I love painting in both oils and watercolours, so teaching art is a real pleasure."

"Presumably, like me, you had to get a stack of qualifications?" Justin asked between mouthfuls of spaghetti.

"Not really. I gained a degree in art and design plus a professional graduate diploma in education, but that's about it, apart from going on a couple of courses. Those basic qualifications have enabled me to teach most forms of painting and drawing. I really enjoy encouraging others to express themselves and bring out their artistic talents."

She was delighted to find that Justin was very interested in photography, sculpture, and ceramics. Omitting to mention her previous work in The Intelligence Corps, Katrina changed the subject to Dream Dates and Friendships. "What do you make of the dating agency?"

"I'm quite impressed with it actually. I thought Melissa Frothington-Smythe was overselling it to me when I registered with her, but it's lived up to most of her claims, though I feared the worst at one stage."

"Oh, why was that?"

"The second date Melissa gave me was a man-eater who I nicknamed Big Bertha because she was big and busty. She bombarded me with text messages after I had tried to let her down lightly. More recently I went to a 'meet and greet' evening which Melissa arranged and found that most of the other ladies were very pleasant. Unfortunately, Big Bertha was also there, and I spent most of the evening trying to detach myself from her. In desperation I went to the loo, but she was waiting for me when I came out."

They both laughed aloud, causing two other diners to look across at them.

"Have you been out with many ladies from the agency?" Katrina asked, after eating the last piece of her steak.

"Five, apart from you. Unfortunately, two of them are no longer with us. You may have read about two of the female members being murdered."

"I did," said Katrina. "You dated them, did you?"

"Yes. One was called Denise and the other Jesse. I only went out with Denise once because we didn't have much in common, but I saw Jesse two or three times. I was shattered when I heard they had both been murdered. What made it worse was that the police regarded me as one of the suspects. But, eventually, they realised their mistake. Anyway, enough of that. What about you? Have you had many dates?"

"You're only the third. There was the stamp collector and a waterboard inspector who talked non-stop about his job."

"So why did such a good-looking woman as you find it necessary to join a dating agency?"

Katrina had already rehearsed her answer. "I'm so busy I don't have much time to socialise."

"Yes," he agreed. "That makes a dating agency such a big advantage, doesn't it?"

Justin paid her further compliments without sounding cheesy, but she was surprised that this tall, imposing man didn't attempt to make a pass at her until he planted a gentle 'goodnight kiss' on her cheek.

By this time he'd walked her to her little blue Volkswagen Beetle, and explained that he was parked nearby. So there was no question of him seeking a lift.

"I enjoyed this evening," he said. "Can we meet up again?"

"Why not? You've got my mobile number – give me a ring."

"Great. Do you like the theatre?"

"Yes."

"Musicals?"

"I love them."

"Well, you might like to come with me next Friday evening to see Cabaret – it's on in Eastbourne after being in the West End."

"OK," she agreed. "It's a date."

CHAPTER SIXTEEN

Friday, 27 September 2013

'This is déjà vu,' thought Boris as Suzie snuggled up to him on her sofa. *'But, hopefully, this time the outcome will be different to the last one!'*

They'd been talking frankly for half an hour in an attempt to sort out their sexual relationship – or lack of one! And Suzie had told him she wanted to try to satisfy him.

It made Boris feel guilty about indulging in his sexual charade with Anna Marie, and he thought how ironic it was that Suzie had not made her offer sooner. *'But perhaps my experience with the prostitute was a good thing – it released my sexual frustrations, and I should now be able to exercise more control over my bloody todger.'*

"Penny for your thoughts," Suzie whispered, kissing him tenderly.

'You would never forgive me if you knew,' he mused. "Nothing, darling. I'm just so pleased you feel you are ready to let me make love to you. Shall we go into the bedroom?"

Suzie took his outstretched hand. As they got to their feet, she wrapped her arms around him. "I do want to please you, darling. I really do."

Boris nuzzled her ear and could smell the sweet floral perfume she'd dabbed there. He found it intoxicating.

After leading her to the bedroom, he kissed her softly on her dimpled cheek. They then lay side by side on top of her bed, fully clothed, cuddling and petting.

Suzie allowed a further tender kiss to develop into a warm, passionate one. As before, Boris's hand stroked her dark brown hair, cheek, and neck. Eventually, it dropped down to touch the outline of one of her breasts, which were hidden beneath a plain blue blouse.

Boris began to get aroused, but this time he made sure the bulge in his trousers didn't press against her.

'I must take things very, very slowly – and certainly not resort to the type of language I used in my role play with Anna Marie.'

Telling Anna Marie to lift her skirt, feel his erection, take down her panties and then suck him off had been the greatest sexual thrill he'd ever known. But to repeat those tactics with Suzie would be a recipe for disaster.

He tried to content himself with rubbing her left breast through her clothing, and was rewarded when Suzie began to undo the buttons of her blouse.

A grateful Boris, fighting to keep his erection under control, brushed his lips against her neck. He then slipped his hand slowly inside the open blouse and eventually moved it along the rim of her pink-trimmed cream bra. He tugged gently at one of the cups, forcing it down so that a delightfully firm bosom fell free. He proceeded to stroke Suzie's ample left breast and nipple, which soon became fully erect.

'She's actually enjoying it, just as she used to do when we had playful fumbles before the assault.'

Suzie gave a pleasurable moan as he bent his head down to suck the large brown nipple.

Boris placed his other hand on her knee. The big test would come when he tried to move it up to her thigh. Would she allow her legs to open slightly for him, or would she shut them tightly?

She did neither. Her legs remained together but not firmly closed. So Boris chanced pushing his hand between them. He got as far as her thighs before she closed them tightly, trapping his probing fingers.

There were more kisses and breast rubbing, but still the path to her panties remained blocked.

"Please, my darling. Please don't deny me now."

Slowly, Suzie allowed her legs to part ever so slightly – just enough for him to advance further.

"I didn't think you liked suspenders," he said, pleasantly surprised.

"I'm wearing them for you, Boris."

Dare he plant her hand on top of his erection? It was a decision he didn't have to make because she took the initiative and started to stroke the fully stretched trouser material covering his bulge with her long, slender fingers.

"Please take me out," Boris begged.

He was in heaven when Suzie pulled down his zip, put her hand delicately inside his trousers, and moved it over his cotton underpants to increase the swelling. There was no need for her to release the penis – it was pushing forward so strongly it popped out through the slit in his pants.

"Darling," he said, "look what you've done to Freddie." This was the name they had used for his tool in the days before sexual interplay between them was ruled out. "Can you see, my darling?"

"Yes."

"Are you pleased you have so much power over him?"

"Yes, I am."

"You're such a clever girl."

"Am I?"

"Yes, you are. I'm so proud of you, Suzie."

"Thank you."

"Do you like playing with Freddie, my darling? Please say you like him."

"Yes, I do," she answered, continuing to caress his bright red weapon.

"Please tell Freddie that you want to be his friend. He's a timid little fellow."

"He's hardly timid or little, darling. But I'll tell him. 'Freddie, I'd like to be your friend.'" As she addressed his tool, she used her index finger and thumb to gently lift it towards her. Suzie resumed stroking the pulsating penis, which became rock hard.

Boris had now pushed his own fingers upwards, inside the pink lace hem of her cream panties. Two of them managed to glide over her pubic hairs and touch her wet lips.

Meanwhile, Suzie rubbed faster.

Boris was ecstatic. *'Is she actually going to let Freddie go inside her for the first time?"*

The question didn't require an answer because the todger was so excited it suddenly erupted, shooting out a stream of creamy liquid over her hand and on the bedspread.

"Oh!" muttered Suzie demurely. "Did I do that to poor Freddie?"

Boris was deflated, both physically and mentally. To make matters worse, he discovered that some of the semen had stained his precious trousers, which were creased around his ankles. He cursed under his breath as he bent to pull up the soiled strides, but when Suzie stroked his face he forced himself to give her a smile.

CHAPTER SEVENTEEN

Monday, 30 September 2013

Katrina received a second visit from Livermore for another briefing. This time she was expecting him and dressed more conservatively in a white polo neck jumper and knee-length blue skirt.

"Well," said Livermore, with a smile after accepting the offer of coffee, "you seem to be getting on nicely with Justin Remington."

"Yes, I am. Were you keeping us under observation all the time we were in Seaford?"

"I certainly was. You and Remington were chatting like old friends while he wined and dined you. I gather he's taking you to the theatre next."

"Yes, we're going to see cabaret at the Congress Theatre, Eastbourne, on Friday night."

"Mrs Livermore won't be too thrilled about your choice of day – October 4th is her birthday, and I was supposed to be taking her out. But keeping you under surveillance is far more important. Buster will actually be in the theatre – one row behind you."

"But I don't even know where we'll be sitting."

"I do. I checked with the box office to find out in which row 'my friend' Justin Remington had booked two tickets, and then reserved one for Buster nearby."

"I'm impressed."

"Is Remington meeting you at the theatre?"

"We're having a drink at the Langham Hotel first."

"So he'll obviously be driving you to the theatre and then dropping you off after the show. Make sure to keep the bugging device in your bag, especially when you're alone in the car with him. You didn't do so until you'd been in the restaurant for over fifteen minutes."

"Sorry about that. I was so nervous I forgot it was in my coat, which one of the staff had hung up . . ."

"It doesn't matter so much in a restaurant or a theatre because it's in public, and I've someone on hand watching you. But it's vital we can hear what's going on when you're alone with Remington. Buster and I will be listening to everything that's said. If you feel in any sort of danger, just say, 'I'm sorry I'm going to sneeze', and Buster will be there within seconds. We'll be sitting in our cars following your every move. Is that OK?"

"Yes. I say 'I'm sorry I'm going to sneeze' if I want help."

"When you're alone with Remington, step up the triple tease. It might help if you dress more provocatively than on your first date."

"Very well."

Livermore exchanged smiles with her. "What has Remington told you about himself?"

"I thought you were listening in to our conversation."

"I couldn't hear everything due to the background noise and the fact you left your phone in the cloakroom for part of the time."

'Touché!' thought Katrina, blushing. "He lives alone and loves music and the arts, especially the theatre. He said he's gone out with five women from the dating agency, including the two who were murdered. He even mentioned that he was one of the suspects until the police realised they had got it wrong."

"He really is a cocky sod and very clever too. Did he say anything more about the women he's dated?"

"He did talk about his second date with a big, busty man-eater who he nicknamed Big Bertha. She fancied him, but he wasn't interested."

"What about the two women who were murdered? Did he tell you anything about them?"

"He mentioned that he went out with Denise only once because they didn't have much in common, and dated Jesse two or three times. Then he changed the subject."

"Surprise, surprise!" Livermore scoffed. "What did he have to say about his work or any of his clients?"

"Not a lot. He merely said he was a financial adviser."

"Failed accountant more like it."

"That's a bit cynical."

"You become cynical in this job, Miss Merton. I've had a bellyful of so-called advisers who rip people off, and cowboys claiming to be decorators."

"Well, I found an excellent painter who did a great job decorating my flat."

"You were lucky. The painter my brother hired overcharged him, left his place in a mess, and went through his wife's knickers drawer. But I digress. Tell me what you make of Remington."

"He's certainly no looker, but he's quite charming. He doesn't strike me as a pervert or a killer. Why are you so certain he murdered those two women?"

"Denise Hollins and Jesse Singleton were sexually assaulted and then stabbed to death in their homes in Brighton. Remington knew how to handle a knife because he did a combat course when he was a reservist with the armed forces a few years ago. He not only admitted to going out with both of the victims very close to the dates they were murdered, but there was forensic evidence connecting him to Jesse Singleton at the scene of the crime."

"So why wasn't that enough to gain a conviction against him?"

Livermore's face creased into a frown. "As I told you previously, it was due to a tech . . ."

"Technicality," Katrina mimicked. She leaned forward in her chair, picked up her cup of coffee from a side table and sipped out of it for several seconds. She was determined not to speak again until he elaborated, and the uncomfortable silence was finally broken by the policeman relenting.

"OK, I'll tell you, but this must be in strict confidence. First, let me emphasis how thorough we were. For example, the victims' fingernails were scraped for any hair, skin, fibres, or material that might have gathered there. The fact we were unable to find any confirmed the victims did not manage to scratch their attacker, no doubt because they were so terrified when he pulled the knife on them that they gave in to his demands.

"Their clothing was examined for traces of bodily fluids such as semen or saliva, and none were discovered. We found nothing at all at the murder scene of Denise Hollins, but in Jesse Singleton's flat was a smashed coffee mug, which could have been handled by the murderer. Unfortunately, the relative who discovered Jesse's body picked up the mug and smudged the fingerprints on it. This relative further contaminated the evidence by placing a sofa cover over the dead body.

"The partial prints were insufficient to give a positive identification but had similarities to Justin Remington's. And we found fibres matching Remington's trousers on the front of the brand-new skirt Jesse Singleton was wearing when she was stabbed."

"That's pretty damning."

"Remington denied being in her flat on the day of the murder, but said he was there two days previously and had sat with her on the sofa. So it was possible that the fibres from his trousers could've been left on the sofa cover previously and then transferred from it to Miss Singleton's skirt. In the absence of conclusive evidence, the Crown Prosecution Service would not agree to the case against Remington going to court."

"In other words, there was reasonable doubt."

"That was what the CPS concluded a jury might think. They were also swayed by the fact that in Remington's role as a financial adviser, he'd visited a company three hours prior to the murder, and his Audi didn't leave the company's car park until after it had been committed."

"That sounds a good alibi to me," Katrina commented, smoothing out a crease in her skirt.

"In theory, yes, but just because his car was on the company's premises most of the day doesn't mean that he was – he could've left on foot and caught a taxi to see Miss Singleton. Or she could've picked him up."

"Wouldn't the company's staff have noticed Justin had gone?"

"Not necessarily. He was working in their archive department on his own for much of the time. I still believed we had enough to charge him and rely on him being caught out under cross-examination in the witness box."

"But according to what I've read, you never found the murder weapon."

"Quite so. That was another factor in the CPS's decision. But I think they allowed themselves to be influenced by what happened in the O. J. Simpson murder investigation."

"How come?"

Livermore obliged her with an explanation. "The O. J. Simpson case was riddled with errors, and the American police were left with egg on their face. One of the mistakes made was that Nicole Brown Simpson's body was covered by an officer with a blanket found inside her condo. This broke a fundamental rule of forensic investigation by disrupting the crime scene – and that was repeated in the case of Jesse Singleton, with the possible transfer of trace evidence."

"Allowing for everything you say, Chief Inspector, the CPS might have been right."

"Wasn't it you, Katrina, who pointed out to me how many times they've got things wrong, as in failing to prosecute Jimmy Savile?"

"Ouch! I fell right into that, didn't I? But Justin could've been telling the truth."

"I don't accept that. Yes, it's possible, but unlikely. For a start, Miss Singleton was wearing a new skirt she had purchased on the morning of her murder. She could have sat in it on the sofa cover herself, but that would not explain how the fibres from Remington's trousers got on the front of the skirt.

"Remington was the obvious suspect. In addition to admitting seeing Miss Singleton on three occasions, he'd also been out with the first victim. The 'clincher' for me was that he had no alibi when the murder of Denise Hollins occurred. We were able to eliminate all our other suspects, including Denise's ex-husband, because they accounted for their whereabouts on the day of her murder – but Remington couldn't. I'm convinced he killed both women."

"And you think I can help you nail him."

"That's right. So don't hold back on the triple tease."

"OK. I'll go braless and flash the teeth, thighs, and tits!"

CHAPTER EIGHTEEN

Friday, 4 October 2013

Cabaret – which starred Will Young as a notorious German nightclub performer in 1931 when Berlin was turned into a sizzling haven of decadence – lived up to Katrina's expectations. The rest of the evening with Justin exceeded them!

As they left the theatre, Katrina was reflecting that Justin had been charming and acted like a perfect gentleman. The only physical contact between them was when he held her arm as they crossed the road.

This was despite her wearing a daring cream dress, with the top parted slightly down the middle from neck to waist, revealing the edges of each breast, and a maxi skirt with a thigh-high split.

'Am I losing my touch?' she pondered. *'Or could it be that I've only flashed the flesh fleetingly when my coat has flapped open? Perhaps a little more teasing is needed.'*

When they were inside Remington's Audi A6, Katrina unbuttoned her coat so that her thigh became clearly visible.

She noticed that Remington's eyes were riveted to the garter near the top of her leg.

While he was distracted, she checked her mobile was in her handbag before placing it on the floor. Katrina then pulled at her coat to restore an air of respectability by making sure her garter was no longer on show.

"That was most enjoyable," she murmured. "The choreography was amazing, and the costumes were dazzling."

"Yes, I thought you'd like it. I've actually seen it before. Not all the songs were memorable, but I loved 'Money Makes the World Go Round' and 'Maybe This Time', and, of course, 'Cabaret'."

They chatted away until they got to where Katrina's car was parked in a side street. Once Justin had turned off the engine, he opened his glove compartment and said, "I've got something for you."

Katrina feared the worst. *'Is he going to get out a knife?'*

Gripped by fear, she tried to say the coded message to summon help but couldn't get the words out.

Justin withdrew something shiny, long, and narrow – but it wasn't a knife. It turned out to be a thin box, wrapped in silver paper. He handed the small package to her.

Katrina made a conscious effort to prevent her hands from shaking as she undid the wrapping. Opening the box, she found it contained a bracelet, from which hung several tiny good luck charms.

"Oh, Justin, you shouldn't have bought me a present."

"I wanted you to know how much I appreciate your company. Let me put it on for you." He removed the bracelet from the box and fitted it to her left wrist, which she'd held out for him.

"It's lovely. Thank you."

Justin moved towards her and planted a gentle kiss on her cheek.

She was so relieved that she responded by brushing her lips lightly against the side of his face. Encouraged, he cupped her chin and kissed her full on the mouth. Katrina backed away, causing his hand to slide from her face and run down the open bodice, touching the outline of her left bosom before he could withdraw it.

"Sorry," he mumbled in response to the look of apprehension on her face.

She observed that he was embarrassed and not showing any signs of lustful intent. In the circumstances, she couldn't imagine him pulling a knife on her.

Katrina reached behind her for the door handle. Then, turning back to face him, she said, "Thank you for a wonderful evening. We must do it again."

*****

"Bloody hell!" raged Bates when he spoke to Livermore after joining him in his car.

"I've been sitting, wasting my time, listening to a lovey-dovey conversation between Katrina and Justin, while wanting to take a pee but unable to leave my fucking car. There's no indication that a rape is going to be committed, Harvey. It's more likely to develop into a big romance."

"Do be patient, Buster. I'll ask Katrina to invite him back to her flat for a coffee on their next date. And when she rejects his advances, he's bound to threaten her."

Buster scratched his brow. "I've been giving some thought to this, Harvey, and I can't get my head around why Katrina would be so willing to help you. Have you got something on her?"

"Why do you say that?"

"The fact that she simply wants to be a good Samaritan following the assault on her sister is one thing. But putting herself at risk by going out with a murder suspect doesn't make sense to me. Unless she's done a deal with you, of course. I need to know what you're getting me into here, mate. You don't suspect she killed Protheroe, do you?"

Livermore hesitated. Then, after several seconds of contemplation, he said, "OK. It might be in both our interests if I tell you the whole story because I know you're a good mate, and I can trust you if I get caught out. But I need you to swear you'll never repeat it unless I ask you to."

"OK, you have my word."

The DCI explained how Katrina's MI5 documents had been stolen in a break-in at her mother's home and he had returned them to her. He went on. "I found it odd that she had left MI5 to work as an art teacher at the same college where her sister had been assaulted in the car park, and her attacker had later been murdered. I wondered if Katrina had been in the Rover in which the rapist was shot. I knew I could find out because after the burglary we'd taken prints of the mother and the two daughters for elimination purposes. So I asked a mate in 'fingerprints' to compare the two sisters' dabs with those found in the Rover."

"Thus flouting police procedures and ignoring citizens' rights to have elimination prints discarded."

Livermore shook his head and cracked his knuckles. "I knew it would be a mistake to tell you."

"Come off it, Harvey. The old knuckles trick doesn't work on me. Now just carry on or I'll be deeply offended."

"Very well. The fingerprint check showed that Suzie was in the clear, but Katrina's prints matched those in the Rover. I was on the point of having Katrina questioned under caution when she approached me and offered to take part in a honeytrap."

"Fucking hell!" exclaimed Buster. "You've compromised your own position and are putting your reputation and career on the line, mate. How do you know you can trust this Katrina? If she's killed once, who's to say she won't kill again, with you her next victim?"

"I must stress, Buster, that she has not admitted to killing Protheroe. She's simply offering me a deal to ensure I don't investigate further what her prints were doing in the Rover. She is terrified of what effect it would have on her already traumatised sister and mother if she was arrested."

"I repeat, Harvey, how do you know she won't drop you in the brown stuff?"

"Katrina's documents, which I saw, show she had an excellent record with MI5 while processing movements of suspected terrorists. I think she can be trusted."

"Processing? You mean she was a glorified clerical officer?"

"It was still a position of trust, Buster, and she was highly commended."

"OK, Harvey. I just hope this doesn't end in disaster."

CHAPTER NINETEEN

Friday, 4 October 2013

Grace Conteh found herself working late on Friday, so she had to cancel her dinner date with Ross Yardley.

She'd looked forward to being wined and dined by the journalist in an exclusive French restaurant but couldn't get there in time for the reservation he'd made.

When Grace phoned Ross at his office to cry off, she simply told him that "something important at work" prevented her seeing him.

"It must be bloody important," he chastised, "to cause us to give up a table in one of Brighton's top eateries."

Grace felt so guilty she made a promise without considering whether she might live to regret it. "I'll make it up to you, Ross. You can come around to my flat one evening, and I'll cook a meal for us."

"When?"

"Well, it had better not be for a few days because I don't know what my boss might have in store for me, and I don't want to risk having to cancel again."

"Are you giving me the brush-off?" Ross asked bluntly.

"No, of course not. I enjoyed meeting you the other night and reminiscing about old times."

"Is that all it was, Grace? Old pals reminiscing?"

"No . . . If you must know, I used to have a 'thing' about you at school."

"Snap," he responded. "All the more reason we should get together."

"How about next Thursday at my flat – say 8 p.m.?"

"Thursday it is," Ross confirmed. "No more cancellations, OK?"

"OK." Throwing caution to the wind, she gave him her address.

CHAPTER TWENTY

Monday, 7 October 2013

Katrina saw Justin again sooner than she'd expected. She and Suzie were almost run over by him on Monday evening as they were walking along Eastbourne seafront on their way to the cinema.

They had paused to cross the road and escape being ogled by two saucy youths, when a bright red Audi flashed past. Suddenly it came to a screeching halt and then backed up until it was alongside them. The male driver wound down his window, stuck out his head, and grinned.

"I'm really getting fed up with these one-track-minded morons coming on to us," muttered Suzie.

But her sister did not reply. Instead, Katrina returned his smile with one of her own.

"Justin!" she gasped. "Is this what you call running into people?"

"Sorry if I startled you, ladies. But I couldn't drive by without saying hello."

When he was introduced to Suzie, he gushed, "Obviously beauty runs in your family."

They exchanged a few further pleasantries before Katrina attempted to bring the conversation to an end.

"Sorry, Justin, but we can't stop. The film we're going to see starts at 8.55, and it's nearly that now."

"Jump in and I'll drop you right outside the cinema," he offered. Within minutes he'd done just that.

"Thank you very much," the sisters chorused as they got out.

"Think nothing of it. Perhaps we can meet up soon, Katrina?"

"That would be nice. Why don't you ring me tomorrow?"

As Justin drove off, waving out of his open window, Katrina could see her sister giving her a strange look.

"What?" she asked.

"Is this guy your new boyfriend?"

"Not exactly . . ."

"You're going out with him, aren't you?"

"Yes," replied Katrina sheepishly.

"I wouldn't have thought he was your type. You usually like the Tom Cruise look, but he's more of an Arnold Schwarzenegger minus some of the muscles and with a lot less hair! Mind you, he is quite well built . . . Has he got a big six-pack?"

"Please don't go on," Katrina pleaded. "It's not what you think. I'll tell you about it sometime. It's a long story."

CHAPTER TWENTY-ONE

Monday, 7 October 2013

While Katrina and Suzie were watching a thriller, there was a real-life drama unfolding in Brighton.

A young couple who'd been out for an Indian meal – and several glasses of wine – were returning to their block of flats in an inebriated state.

"That wine was powerful stuff," said the mini-skirted girl called Paula, giggling. "It's made me quite woozy. I'm not feeling myself."

"You can leave that job to me," joked her piece of rough. "I'm going to feel you all over and then shag you senseless."

"It all depends if I can stop myself throwing up," Paula replied, almost tripping over the doormat in the porch. She clung on to his arm as they shakily approached the lift.

Her outstretched hand didn't succeed in making contact with the buzzer, so the pockmarked youth named George pressed it for her. They waited in vain despite him pushing the buzzer three more times.

"Blasted lift must be stuck or out of order," George moaned. "We'll have to take the stairs."

They started to stagger up the nearby staircase towards her fourth-floor flat, with Paula holding on to him for support.

"I hope I'm not going to be sick," she said.

On reaching the second floor they decided to quickly check the lift again but were halted in their tracks by the sight that greeted them.

Both the metal lift doors were partly open because lying on the floor between them, half in and half out of the elevator, was the body of a woman. There was blood everywhere.

"Oh shit!" shrieked Paula before finally vomiting.

CHAPTER TWENTY-TWO

Monday, 7 October 2013

Livermore had learned how to keep his temper in the face of severe provocation by some really obnoxious criminals, but he was in danger of losing it with his wife's know-it-all sixty-seven-year-old aunt Hilda.

He and Agnes were visiting her aunt and uncle in the old couple's bungalow in Langney, on the outskirts of Eastbourne, and Harvey had been persuaded, against his better judgement, to join them in a game of whist.

Uncle Maurice, obviously knowing what was in store, tried to opt out and suggested that they use a dummy hand instead of involving him, but his wife wouldn't hear of it. And Livermore soon discovered that the real dummy was headstrong Aunt Hilda! She mistakenly believed she was a good card player. This certainly wasn't the case, and Livermore found that partnering her was a nightmare.

He'd been dealt some terrible cards, and Hilda's errors added to his frustration. To make matters worse, she stubbornly refused to admit to her mistakes and instead exclaimed, "There's no use pulling a face, Harvey. I have to play according to my hand."

When he tried to explain something to her, she would fiddle with her hearing aid and claim it wasn't working. Maurice raised his right hand to his forehead in an apparent gesture of mock disbelief and, upon being spotted doing so by his wife, used the hand to swat a non-existent fly.

Harvey's luck was finally about to change when he had a good hand for once and his partner Hilda was all smiles, inferring she did too. Hearts were trumps, and it transpired that Hilda had five of them, but she promptly threw away her advantage. When spades were played for the first time, she trumped in with an ace instead of using a low heart. She then led the king of clubs and had it taken by the ace, having done the same thing with the king of diamonds in the previous hand. And to cap it all, she overtrumped Livermore when he had a trick won.

"I'd already got that, Auntie," he said, failing to mask his annoyance.

"I have to play according to my hand," Hilda exclaimed for the umpteenth time.

Livermore winced as Agnes kicked him under the table. "Harvey, don't talk to Auntie like that," she scolded.

He resisted the temptation to throw in his cards. *'It's only a game,'* he kept telling himself, but playing with two strong-willed ladies was testing his patience severely.

Livermore just wished that his misery would end – and suddenly it did. His mobile phone rang. He quickly took the call and announced he must leave.

"Really, Harvey!" complained his wife. "That's nae right. We're in a middle of a game."

"I've got to go," Livermore said emphatically. "There's been a murder. And that takes priority – even over a game of whist with you and your aunt."

CHAPTER TWENTY-THREE

Monday, 7 October 2013

The quiet Brighton street containing the block of flats in which the dead woman's body had been found was soon disturbed by the arrival of police cars and a swarm of officers.

DS Chris Dimbleby and DC Conteh were tasked with interviewing a clearly stressed-out George Fitch and Paula Crouch, who threw up again between sobs.

Livermore and Nottage donned white protective clothing and shoe covers so that they could view the victim's body without contaminating the scene with their own DNA or transferring materials from other locations.

Even the experienced Livermore was badly affected by what he saw. The gaping wound in the dead woman's throat had caused her white designer dress to be covered in large red patches by the outpouring blood, which had splattered on to the floor, walls, and ceiling. There was also a deep cut to her right hand. She appeared to have been in her late twenties and probably quite attractive, but her features now looked distorted.

The whole area had been sealed off by strips of blue and white tape. A police photographer was clicking away as three members of the Scenes of Crime team meticulously dusted surfaces for prints, most of which were not visible to the naked eye, and gathered evidence in clear plastic bags, to be sealed airtight.

Eventually, Livermore and Nottage were able to consult forensic pathologist Stefan Gilchrist and Scenes of Crime Officer Neville Kilby. They huddled together on the second floor landing outside the victim's one-bedroom flat, which was three doors from the lift.

"So?" Livermore asked. "What can you tell me?"

"She was killed by a deep knife wound to the throat – probably sometime in the last four hours," Gilchrist responded.

"What else?"

"Well," said Kilby, "there are no signs of the door to her flat being forced, so it would seem she let the murderer in, indicating that she knew him."

"What about inside the flat?" queried Nottage, taking off his glasses and using his handkerchief to wipe clean the lenses, which had become misty.

"There are a few indications of a disturbance in the lounge where the table lamp was knocked over. When my team has finished their examination, I may know more."

An impatient Livermore wanted some answers now. "Do you think this could've been done by the same man who murdered Denise Hollins and Jesse Singleton?"

Kilby, a fifty-year-old throwback to the sort of colourful characters who pop up in television dramas such as *Midsomer Murders,* and Gilchrist, a slightly younger, less-outgoing, smaller individual, both said it was too early to give a definite opinion.

"Of course, the method of killing was different," reflected Gilchrist. "The first two victims had a knife thrust through their third and fourth ribs to puncture the thin-walled ventricle of the heart. It resulted in almost instant death and limited blood loss. This time the victim's throat was slit, and there's a mass of blood, but on all three occasions, the perpetrator demonstrated that he knew how to kill with a single slash."

"So it could be the same man," Livermore concluded. "He presumably found it necessary to use a different method because this lady was fleeing."

"Yes," agreed Gilchrist. "To stop her escaping, or crying out for help, he resorted to cutting her throat. She was obviously trying to shield herself because her right hand was sliced to the bone. As with the previous murders, the cuts were deep and wide, so it could have been the same knife – a long, double-edged blade."

"Poor little cow," said Nottage. "She didn't stand a chance against this butcher."

"But, as before, there's no sign of the knife," Kilby interjected. "It's unfortunate he didn't panic and leave it behind."

Livermore looked quizzically from the SOCO to the pathologist. Gilchrist told him, "The killer may have literally slipped up this time by leaving two partial footprints. He must have trod in his victim's blood. It caused him to slide, so the footprints are far from perfect, but even so, they may be enough to help us discover the type, make, description, and approximate size."

"That could give us our first break," Livermore acknowledged. "But were there any other similarities with the previous murders?"

"Yes," said Gilchrist. "In addition to their fatal wounds, all three victims had small cuts under the chin, which suggests that the knife was initially held there by the killer to try to make the women comply with his wishes. He used just enough pressure to draw a trace of blood from their chins. But while the first two women had underwear ripped and tears or swelling around the anus, caused by the probable insertion of a blunt instrument, this lady did not appear to suffer such indignities. I'd stress, however, that any conclusions at this stage would be pure speculation."

"So let's speculate!" urged Livermore. "I see two possible scenarios. This lady could've had consensual sexual contact with the killer until he revealed he wanted to shove something up her back passage and threatened her with the knife, causing her to flee. But the more likely alternative is that she refused any form of sex and caught the attacker off guard by pushing him over or giving him a knee in the nuts before running out."

Gilchrist nodded. "Either of those scenarios would explain why there's no apparent sign of anal entry this time. But you'll have to wait until after the post-mortem to be sure."

"One other thing . . .," Kilby volunteered. "The victim was sexually active. You should see the stuff in her bedside cabinet – there's quite a collection."

Livermore was about to reply when DS Michael O'Sullivan approached him.

Ignoring Nottage, O'Sullivan told the chief, "We've confirmed the identity of the victim and a few details about her, Gov. Her name was Zena Cattermole, and among her identity cards is one marked 'DDFI'."

"DDFI?"

"Dream Dates and Friendships Incorporated. She was a member of the same dating agency as the other two victims."

CHAPTER TWENTY-FOUR

Monday, 7 October 2013

The feelings of anger sometimes became unbearable, particularly when the voices in his head taunted him.

He had begun hearing them as a schoolboy. They would tell him to do dreadful things to his strict English teacher, Miss Stonehouse. "Stab her hand with your pen" and "Push her down the stairs," they would say. It had taken considerable willpower to avoid carrying out such acts of violence.

He had not shown the same degree of resistance when the voices told him to imagine Miss Stonehouse in her underwear and to spy on the third-year girls' hockey team taking their showers.

By the start of his teens he'd became eaten up with sexual frustration. For this he could blame his awful step-parents who'd repeatedly molested him.

They had been freakish in every way, including the 'looks' department, with his stepmother being afflicted by an ugly wart on her pointed chin and his stepfather having a bulbous nose spouting more hairs than he had on his head.

But their habits were far more revolting. Not content with buggering him, they performed crude sexual acts in his presence before pushing him away and ridiculing him.

They were monsters – and he grew into one too.

The voices became more frequent, yet at least they offered a weird form of companionship. On the days they were not messing with his head, he felt completely alone and unwanted. It probably stemmed from the fact his real mother had turned her back on him, but not on his brothers.

His intense jealousy and resentment of his brothers was matched by the contempt and loathing he felt for his mother. "She should have kept me and given away one of the others," he would mutter through his burning anger and tears.

The result of all these traumas was a lethal cocktail – his increasing desire for rough sex, coupled with a growing hatred of rejection.

When he was refused by women, he simply lost control. It wasn't his fault – the demons inside his head were to blame!

Now they had caused him to kill this 'silly cow' Zena, and he was desperate to wash her blood from his hands and clothing.

CHAPTER TWENTY-FIVE

Tuesday, 8 October 2013

Livermore, having not got home until 3 a.m., snatched four hours' sleep and was back in Sussex House in time to call a meeting of the major crime team early Tuesday morning.

The incident room was buzzing with a sense of resolve and purpose to find the killer as more than thirty officers, mainly plain clothed, took their seats. Office Manager DS Len Bridger was standing, grim-faced, at the back, while Mike O'Sullivan was perched on the edge of a desk, sipping coffee in between scoffing a sandwich that he'd just purchased from a nearby greasy spoon.

"For those who don't already know, let me update you by telling you that the woman who was murdered last night was called Zena Cattermole," Livermore began. "She was a thirty-year-old interior designer, single, and lived on her own. From what we found in her bedroom, she would appear to have led a very active sex life – there's a variety of condoms and lubricants plus a collection of sex toys, including a cane and handcuffs."

"A regular Miss Whiplash," declared O'Sullivan.

"Yet, according to her mother, Miss Cattermole was a very respectable woman," Nottage chipped in. "Conteh and I have spoken to her briefly, and we'll be seeing her again. Unfortunately, she and her daughter had not been in regular contact recently."

The chief inspector had already put up pictures of Zena Cattermole on a large white noticeboard. Three were crime scene photos showing her mutilated body at different angles, and two more were snapshots from the woman's photo album.

Livermore stressed that the attractive blonde, who'd looked much younger than her thirty years, had a lot in common with the two previous victims. He then recounted the similarities in this murder and those of Denise Hollins and Jesse Singleton before drawing a conclusion. "I believe they were committed by the same man, and we're looking for a serial killer. The fact that all three women were members of the Dream Dates and Friendships dating agency is particularly significant."

"That puts Justin Remington back in the frame then," said Nottage.

"Yes, it does. He was, of course, a member of the same agency and went out with the previous two victims. It won't surprise me if we learn he also dated Miss Cattermole. We'll be having him in for questioning today."

"What about motive?" asked Chris Dimbleby, peering from behind the computer on the desk in front of him. The detective sergeant – a cynical, long-serving officer with an old-school mentality who'd twice been passed over for promotion – continued, "Should we assume it was purely a sexual attack in all three cases?"

"There could be several possible motives," replied Livermore. "The psychological profile of the killer in the previous two murders implied he's a psychopath driven by sexual desire, power, control, and possibly anger at being rejected . . ."

"That doesn't sound like Remington to me," Dimbleby cut in. "The killer could be a weirdo who just picks on women at random."

"I didn't know you held an advanced degree in psychology, Chris," scoffed O'Sullivan.

Livermore waited for the laughter to die down before continuing, "Actually, Chris, you have a point. Although the evidence suggests it's the same man, it might not be wise for us to jump to conclusions because that could send us in the wrong direction. But do I need to remind you the majority of murders are committed by people known to their victims? That also applies to a large number of rapes. There's little chance the three murder victims would all have let a man into their homes unless they knew him. And it's surely more than coincidence that all three were members of the same dating agency. It's odds on that's how the killer first came into contact with them."

There were murmurs of agreement.

"I know we vetted all the Dream Dates male members after the first two murders, but now we need to run checks on them again – particularly those who went out with Miss Cattermole. Can you take care of organising that, Mike?"

O'Sullivan almost choked on the remains of his sandwich. "Consider it done, Gov. I'll get the names of every bloke who received her details from the agency."

Livermore resumed addressing his team. "Our killer was too clever to leave any traces of semen, blood, saliva, or any other DNA at the scenes of the first two murders, but this time, with the victim trying to flee, he may've made a mistake. If forensics comes up with any of his DNA, or fibres from his clothes, on Miss Cattermole or in her flat, then we've got the bastard. But I'm taking nothing for granted until I get the full scene-of-crime report and the post-mortem result.

"So, Chris, bearing in mind your earlier point, can you check the Sex Offenders Register again to see how many offenders currently living in the area are unable to account for what they were doing last night?"

"Certainly, Gov. I'll . . ."

He was interrupted by his own mobile bleeping to signal he had a message, which he promptly relayed. "Gov, the set of car keys we found in Miss Cattermole's flat was for a Fiat in one of the parking bays. Forensics are going through it."

"Good," acknowledged Livermore. His brow then furrowed as he tried to regain his train of thought. "The initial indication is that the time of death was after 8 p.m. and before 9.30 p.m., which was when a young couple, George Fitch and Paula Crouch, literally stumbled across the body. We may be able to narrow it down even more when we find out the last time Miss Cattermole was seen alive or was talking on the phone. And surely someone must've heard her cry out for help. I want all the residents in her block of flats interviewed, together with neighbours from adjoining properties. Jeff, you're already organising the door-to-door calls, aren't you?"

"Yes, Gov."

"We need to learn as much about Zena Cattermole as possible. Grace, you go through her diary, address book, and telephone records and draw up a list. There were some messages on her answerphone, including one from a man called Carl who seemed to be on very friendly terms with her. See if his contact details are in her address book."

"I'll get straight on to it," Conteh responded, looking up from her notebook in which she'd been scribbling frantically. "Can I ask a question, Gov?"

"Fire away, Constable."

"Well, you believe the same man killed all three women. But it seems strange that the first two murders occurred just a month apart, yet there has been a gap of four months between the second and third murders. And doesn't the fact that Zena had her throat cut suggest we could be looking for a different murderer?"

"I don't think so. The reason why the killer slashed the throat instead of stabbing his victim this time was because the circumstances were different. He had to chase after Miss Cattermole, as she ran out of her flat to the lift. There are enough similarities to make me believe it's the same man."

"And it's all pointing to Remington," O'Sullivan concluded.

"Yes, but just because he's our main suspect certainly doesn't mean we should overlook any other possible candidates. I want full checks carried out on everyone else who knew Zena, including this guy Carl, for example. DI Nottage is the deputy senior investigating officer, so report to him if I'm not available. And let's not rule anyone out at this stage. It could be . . ."

A phone rang at the back of the room and DS Bridger answered it. He put his hand over the mouthpiece and called to Livermore, "It's the press, Gov. What shall I tell them?"

"Nothing," snapped the chief inspector.

After Bridger had rang off, Livermore instructed, "I want all calls from the media to be referred to our Press Bureau. Under no circumstances tell anyone that all three victims had cuts under their chins or the knife used on all of them had a long double-edged blade. We want to hold back that sort of information, as it might help us to trap the killer – and should also enable us to quickly eliminate those time-wasting attention-seekers who love confessing to a murder they didn't commit.

"The last thing I want is loads of cranks claiming they are the serial killer and causing us to waste countless hours checking them out. Have you all got that?"

There was a chorus of affirmatives. Conteh's cry of "Understood, Gov" came over the loudest.

But the DCI had a premonition that this case was going to be a nightmare.

CHAPTER TWENTY-SIX

Tuesday, 8 October 2013

After an uneventful morning Livermore got the first breakthrough he was seeking when O'Sullivan phoned, following his visit to Dream Dates and Friendships.

"I've spoken to the dating agency's matchmaker, a stuck-up cow called Melissa Frothington-Smythe. Would you believe that she tried to sign me up as a client and offered me a free trial? Anyway, I got from her the names of the male members for whom she arranged dates with Zena Cattermole."

"And did they include Justin Remington?"

"No, Gov. Remington wasn't among them, but he was at a social function the agency put on. And surprise, surprise, Zena also attended it."

"So he did know her!" Livermore boomed, unable to keep the excitement out of his voice.

"Yes. Melissa remembers seeing Remington and Zena chatting at this 'meet and greet' evening. She also recalls them dancing together. Zena may've given him her phone number – they could've arranged their own date."

"Very interesting. Well done, Mike."

The DCI was even more elated when he received another phone call, this time from Nottage.

"Good news, Gov. One of our door-knocking team has been speaking to a lady called Dawn Smithson who lives on the same floor as Miss Cattermole did. She says she was returning home just after 8.15 p.m. last night and noticed a man ringing the bell of Miss Cattermole's flat. She had to pass by to get to her own flat at No. 45, so she saw Miss Cattermole open the door of No. 39 to him. Miss Smithson remembers looking at her clock when she went into her flat, and it was 8.20. This, of course, was only seventy minutes before the body was found. So we now know the murder was committed between 8.20 p.m. and 9.30 p.m. That narrows it down considerably."

"Does this neighbour remember what the man looked like?"

"She does. She only got a side view of him, and he was wearing a hat, but her description matches that of Justin Remington."

CHAPTER TWENTY-SEVEN

Tuesday, 8 October 2013

Late on Tuesday Livermore finally received a preliminary report from the lab liaison officer that incorporated Stefan Gilchrist's findings following the post-mortem.

He went through it immediately and was disappointed to see that most of the initial indications were unhelpful.

There were no signs that Zena Cattermole had been sexually assaulted or indulged in intercourse just before her death, dashing hopes of discovering sperm or pubic hair belonging to her murderer.

But after ploughing through some technical jargon in the report, Livermore focused on two paragraphs that caused his eyes to light up with delight.

The first referred to traces of dried semen being found on the bed sheets in the victim's flat, implying she'd had sex recently. Another discovery was three short, dark brown head hairs, one of which still had the follicle attached. They were among many strands of Miss Cattermole's own blonde hair on her bloodstained dress.

Livermore phoned the lab liaison officer and asked him to compare the samples with those taken from Justin Remington following the previous two murders that had involved a mouth swab and his hairs being collected from a brush.

*****

Wednesday, 9 October 2013

A phone call from Nottage brought more good news. CCTV footage showed a man, closely resembling Remington, walking quickly towards the victim's block of flats shortly before the 8.20 p.m. sighting by the neighbour.

"The man's facial features are not clear, and he was wearing a hat, but it's a good likeness to Remington," Nottage enthused. "And it ties in with the neighbour's description."

"Well, it looks like I've got you this time, matey," Livermore said to himself.

Another phone call caused the chief inspector to rub his hands together in satisfaction – the footprints at the crime scene suggested they were from a man's size 11 shoes with leather soles. And Livermore already knew that Remington wore 11s.

He was sufficiently encouraged to ring his senior officer and provide him with an update.

Normally, he tried to give as little information as possible to his fastidious taskmaster, known throughout the Sussex force as 'Fussy Frampton'. But this was different – he was about to arrest Remington on suspicion of murder.

It was time to play it by the book after keeping quiet about the unorthodox undercover scheme to try to draw Remington into a honeytrap. If Detective Superintendent Frampton knew how Livermore had plotted with Katrina Merton, a murder suspect, in an attempt to trap another likely murderer, the DS would have him suspended, prosecuted, and probably locked up!

No way would Frampton have tolerated the 'set a thief to catch a thief' plan.

The dates with Katrina had not produced anything anyway, but soon there should be enough evidence to charge Remington with the latest murder, as Livermore was quick to inform 'Fussy'.

"That's exactly what you told me after the two previous murders," Frampton pointed out. "The CPS disagreed – so you'd better be 100 per cent sure this time, Harvey."

"I can't be certain until I get the full lab reports, sir. I'm waiting to find out if three brown hairs found on Zena Cattermole and semen discovered on her bed sheet belonged to Remington. But there's other evidence.

"As with the previous two murders, Remington again knew the victim – they all belonged to the same dating agency. And a neighbour, Dawn Smithson, saw a man calling at Zena Cattermole's flat shortly before her murder took place – the description she's given matches Remington. CCTV also shows a man resembling Remington walking towards the block of flats a few minutes before that."

There was a pause at the other end of the line. Then Frampton's cultured tones sounded a note of caution. "We must wait to discover if the hairs are a match. Let's see what the forensics report says after a full analysis has been made, and then I'll review the evidence before submitting it to the CPS. Send me details of everything."

"With all due respect, sir, this serial killer could strike again if we don't nick him."

"He can't while you're questioning him, can he? So go ahead and arrest him, search his property, and bring in every pair of shoes the bugger possesses, but make sure you dot the i's and cross the t's. Arrange a video identity parade and see if the neighbour picks him out. If she does, and we subsequently find that the hairs match or there's blood on his shoes, then the CPS should accept we have an excellent case – providing, of course, that Remington doesn't come up with an alibi."

Livermore's earlier elation was beginning to fade. He doubted if Remington would agree to take part in an ID parade and feared that, if he did, Dawn Smithson might pick the wrong man because she'd only got a side view of the caller. He was certain Remington would have thrown his blood-covered shoes and clothing away, and had to accept that the CCTV footage on its own would probably not be conclusive.

He cracked his knuckles in annoyance. *'It will be a bloody travesty if the bastard escapes being charged again.'*

CHAPTER TWENTY-EIGHT

Wednesday, 9 October 2013

Much to Livermore's surprise, Remington readily consented to a video identity parade.

"Nobody can pick me out as being at the crime scene because I simply wasn't there," he insisted.

But as this would take time to arrange, Livermore's immediate concern was what Remington had to say for himself when questioned.

The interview with him proved completely frustrating for Nottage and Conteh because his solicitor, a Rottweiler of a woman in both manner and looks called Muriel Bellington, kept interrupting.

Acting under her advice, Remington issued a string of denials while limiting himself to 'yes' and 'no' answers whenever possible.

Livermore, having watched the whole charade on a computer screen in his office, was on his way to finding Nottage when his old adversary Bellington caught up with him in the corridor.

"Good morning, Chief Inspector. I must express my concern to you. You guys have got it all wrong again," she growled.

"That's what you claimed when we arrested your last client – until you realised he'd been caught red-handed on camera," Livermore shot back.

"Well, this time it's different, isn't it? I presume that none of the Automatic Number Plate Recognition Cameras on the routes to Brighton have shown any signs of Mr Remington's car on the evening of the murder."

"That's easily explained, Ms Bellington. He could've already been in Brighton or travelled there by train – or in another car."

"No. It's explained by the fact he wasn't there at all. This has become a witch-hunt. You previously tried without success to charge Mr Remington for the murders of Denise Hollins and Jesse Singleton. Even the CPS rejected your so-called evidence. Now you've arrested him for the murder of a third woman purely because they all belonged to the same dating agency."

"If our roles were reversed, you'd have arrested him too, Muriel."

She treated him to a frosty smile, which seemed more like a glare. "I understand that brown hairs were found on the victim's bloodstained dress. Even if they turn out to be my client's, that won't prove anything. Mr Remington admits to having met

Zena Cattermole and dancing with her at a recent social event. Strands of his hair could easily have become mingled with hers and then got transferred to her dress. Once again the police case is flawed. I'll be carefully studying every piece of your paperwork relating to my client being arrested. It doesn't smell right to me."

'*Trust you to bring smells into it,*' thought Livermore, suppressing a smile. '*After all, Rottweilers are known for their strong sense of smell.*' He imaged her on all fours, sniffing around, but somehow managed to keep a straight face and confined himself to saying, "Be that as it may, I believe there'll be sufficient evidence for a charge to be made."

CHAPTER TWENTY-NINE

Wednesday, 9 October 2013

Katrina was surprised not to receive a phone call from Justin, but on Wednesday she got one from Livermore.

"You'll be pleased to know that you have no need to go out on any more dates with Justin Remington," the chief inspector informed her.

"Why's that?"

"We've arrested him in relation to the murder of a third victim, and he's currently in police custody."

"I find that hard to accept. If he's a killer, he deserves an Oscar. He acted like a perfect gentleman when he was with me. He certainly didn't show any signs of being a sex maniac or a crazed murderer."

"Perhaps he's schizophrenic. As I told you, Katrina, I was convinced he'd killed two women already, and now he's murdered a third called Zena Cattermole. This time he slit her throat."

"How awful! I read about her murder in today's paper. She was also a member of Dream Dates, wasn't she?"

"That's right. Remington wasn't content with just going out with you – he must have fancied her as well. Fortunately, he never tried to attack you, but Zena wasn't so lucky. We believe Remington attempted to sexually molest her in her lounge, but instead of succumbing to his threats, she ran out of her flat. She was trying to escape via the lift when he knifed her."

"Why are you so sure Justin did it? Does he admit it?"

"He denies even being with Zena, but he was seen calling at her flat by one of her neighbours shortly before she was killed."

"When did the murder happen exactly?"

"On Monday night, between 8.20 p.m. and 9.30 p.m., in Brighton. Zena opened her door to the man answering Remington's description at 8.20, and her body was discovered by a young couple just over an hour later. Everything points to Remington."

Katrina was suddenly consumed by a mixture of shock and puzzlement. "You've got it wrong. It wasn't him."

"What do you mean?"

"It couldn't have been Justin because my sister and I ran into him when we were on our way to the cinema on Monday evening. Or, to be more accurate, he almost ran into us in his car."

"What!" Livermore exploded. "That's impossible."

"I'm sorry, but it's true. We bumped into him in Eastbourne at no later than 8.45 p.m., and we chatted for fully five minutes."

"You must have got your times wrong."

"No. I remember telling him that we had to dash because the film my sister and I were going to see started at 8.55, so we had only a few minutes left to get to the cinema. He offered to give us a lift in his Audi and dropped us off with only a minute or two to spare. So there's no way he could've been 25 miles away in Brighton at the times you say. Even if he'd driven like mad, he couldn't have got to Brighton until after the body was found."

"I don't believe this," groaned the policeman, raising his voice. "You offered to go out with Remington in order to trap him – instead, you've given him an alibi to get him off."

CHAPTER THIRTY

Wednesday, 9 October 2013

After his telephone conversation with Katrina, a disgruntled Livermore called Nottage into his office to give him an update – and use him as a sounding board.

What Livermore particularly liked about the bright young inspector was that he was not a 'yes man'. He came up with some good ideas and wasn't afraid to express them, even if they contradicted the views of his boss. But, unlike the outspoken Dimbleby, whose nickname 'Dim' was often appropriate, Nottage engaged his brain before opening his mouth.

"So the fact that Katrina and Suzie Merton were with Remington in Eastbourne up to 8.53 p.m. proves that he couldn't have been in Brighton killing Zena Cattermole," the senior policeman lamented. "This is backed up by the fact there's no sign of his car on the ANPR cameras on the routes from Eastbourne to Brighton."

"Perhaps he went around the back roads and the Merton sisters got their timings wrong, Gov. Even a few minutes would make a big difference. I think it would still have been possible for Remington to do it."

Livermore was adamant. "What's now indisputable is that Remington was not the man picked up by CCTV near Miss Cattermole's flat and to whom she opened her door at around 8.20. The only way he could've been that man was if he'd killed her as soon as he arrived at her flat and then raced to Eastbourne immediately afterwards. But he'd have needed to do the journey in record time and would've been covered in blood – the Merton sisters could not have failed to notice that. So the bloke who was at Miss Cattermole's flat at 8.20 was someone else and must also be a suspect."

"Agreed, Gov. But our mystery man could've departed before Remington arrived. If Katrina Merton is slightly mistaken with the time she's given, and Remington left her five minutes earlier, he could've put his foot down and been in Brighton 35 minutes later at around 9.23. The couple who discovered the body might have done so slightly later than they thought. That would be quite possible because they didn't make a 999 call until 9.38 p.m."

Livermore found himself doing something he never thought he ever would – defending the man he'd been pursuing. "But allowing the minimum possible amount of time that Paula Crouch would've spent throwing up and being comforted by her boyfriend, the very latest they could've discovered the body would've been 9.33 p.m. – five minutes before ringing 999. It wouldn't have left Remington long enough to get there and do it."

"I think it would, Gov. Let's assume he made it by 9.23 p.m. That would've left him ten minutes – enough time to go into Zena's flat, threaten her with a knife, chase after her, kill her at the lift entrance, and make his escape."

"No," Livermore corrected. "It would've been far less than ten minutes – more like six. You're not taking account of the fact that the lift was out of action, so he would've had to go down two flights of stairs BEFORE Paula Crouch and George what's-his-name came stumbling up them. They insist nobody went past them, and they saw nobody, so we're actually talking about from the time they came into the building, which would've been 9.29 p.m. at the latest if we assume it took them at least four minutes to climb the stairs. That would've given Remington just six minutes. And that's not realistic, especially bearing in mind the Merton sisters say he showed no signs of being in a hurry when he gave them a lift in Eastbourne. If we . . ."

He was interrupted by his phone ringing. Livermore picked it up and sighed on hearing the unsettling tones of his agitated wife Agnes at the other end.

"Harvey," said the Scottish voice, "I cannae find your best suit, and you need to wear it to the wedding on Saturday. What on earth have you done with it?"

Blast,' thought the police chief. *'I'd completely forgotten about our nephew's wedding.'*

"Sorry. Is the wedding THIS Saturday?"

"Aye, it is, Harvey! Don't you dare tell me you cannae come."

"I'm fully intending to be at the wedding, dear – unless, of course, another murder is committed in the meantime."

"If you don't come, then there will be a murder committed – by ME! And it will be YOURS!"

"I don't think that will be necessary," replied Livermore, hoping desperately that Nottage couldn't hear his wife's threats. "Now I must press on."

"What about your best suit? Where is it?"

"I don't know," he replied, rubbing his fingers over his now-aching temple. "Are you sure you didn't take it to the cleaners after I wore it to that annual dinner last month?"

There was a silence at the other end of the phone.

"Are you still there, Agnes?"

"Aye."

"Perhaps you took it to the cleaners and forgot you'd done so," the policeman suggested, reaching in his desk drawer and pulling out a bottle of aspirin.

"Aye, perhaps I did," Agnes conceded in her broad Scottish accent, which was always more pronounced when she was forced to admit she might be wrong.

Livermore, trying to unscrew the bottle one-handed, dropped it on the floor, causing several of the tablets to spill out. "Damn and blast it!"

"Don't you swear at me, Harvey!" Agnes exploded.

"I wasn't talking to you, dear. I just dropped something on the floor. Now I must go. Goodbye."

Before she could speak again he hung up the phone. He felt embarrassed at being scolded by his wife in front of a colleague, but, fortunately, he didn't have to make immediate eye contact with Nottage. The young DI was bending down, picking up the tablets off the floor. He placed them on the table without comment. When their eyes did meet, Nottage gave his boss what he took to be a sympathetic grin.

Livermore grasped two of the aspirin in his shaking fingers and gulped them down. "Now where was I? Ah, yes. If we presented your scenario in court, the defence counsel would rip us to pieces, especially as it normally takes more than forty minutes to drive to Brighton from Eastbourne. Even accepting the murder scene was outside the town centre, that's at least thirty-five minutes."

Nottage shook his head, causing his glasses to slip slightly down his nose. Pushing them back, he asked, "What if the hairs on the victim's dress are Remington's?"

"His solicitor reckons that would only prove he'd been with Zena Cattermole some time previously – not when the murder was committed. I don't buy that for one moment. But now that the Merton sisters have given Remington an alibi and his car is not shown on ANPR cameras, we can't hold him."

"It doesn't make sense, Gov. But I suppose we now have to concentrate on looking for the man who arrived at Miss Cattermole's flat at 8.20."

"That's right. O'Sullivan is checking up on other Dream Dates members who went out with her. We could be looking for a second mystery man. There was a framed picture of Miss Cattermole with some unknown guy, presumably a boyfriend, on her windowsill. The dating agency have confirmed he wasn't one of their members, so who the bloody hell is he?"

"The man who visited her flat at 8.20?"

"Maybe – maybe not. We also need to find out if it was him or someone else who had sex with Miss Cattermole recently. No semen was found in vaginal swabs taken from her, but there was semen on the sheets of her bed. If, as Remington insists, it wasn't his, whose was it?"

What Nottage said next caught Livermore off guard. "I can't help wondering if Katrina Merton isn't mixed up in this."

"What do you mean, Jeff?"

"Well, her name keeps cropping up, doesn't it? For starters, Katrina used the same college car park where her sister Suzie was assaulted and where the probable rapist, Hugo Protheroe, was subsequently murdered in a Rover. The Rover's owner told us he has no recollection of ever giving Katrina a lift, and I've discovered that none of the other known drivers of the car recalled doing so either. It's worth checking if either of the sisters' prints matches those of the unidentified dabs in the car."

Livermore cursed under his breath that his officers were sometimes too sharp for their own good – and his! *Damn it. Nottage has come to the same conclusion as me. I must be mad to have involved Katrina Merton. I'm so determined to prove Remington is a murderer and stop him from killing again that I'm breaking every bloody rule in the book – and I could be rumbled.'*

But he said non-committally, "The initial investigation into Protheroe's murder showed many people had been in that old Rover. It was probably driven by several of the owner's friends, so they could've given a lift to a lot of other people, including the Merton sisters, at some time. Most of the names have been logged, but there were a couple of occasions when five or six passengers crammed into the car and not all of them could be remembered. Therefore, if either of the sisters' prints is in the car, it's not conclusive."

Nottage didn't look completely convinced, so Livermore reinforced his point. "Don't get sidetracked, Jeff. Your time will be better spent helping to track down the pervert who's killing these women."

CHAPTER THIRTY-ONE

Thursday, 10 October 2013

Livermore's bad mood had not improved when Katrina and her sister came in to write statements the next morning.

Nottage was not available, as he was in court giving evidence in a long-running fraud case in which he'd been the investigating arresting officer prior to transferring to the major crime team, so the sisters were greeted by O'Sullivan.

He took Suzie's statement, and Katrina gave hers to Dimbleby. Katrina was then shown into Livermore's office while her sister waited for her in reception.

"Where does this leave us?" Katrina asked the chief inspector as he looked through her account of how Remington had run into the sisters in Eastbourne at possibly the same time the latest murder had occurred in Brighton.

"I take it you're referring to our agreement that I would not look further into your possible involvement in the murder of one pervert if you assisted me in putting another behind bars," he said, glancing up at her. "But, far from helping me convict Remington, you've caused me to set him free. I wouldn't call that honouring your part of the bargain, would you?"

"That's very unfair, Chief Inspector. I couldn't withhold that I saw Justin Remington, could I? It actually proves he did not kill this latest victim."

"We'll be checking out the timings. But the fact remains he could've murdered two of the previous women he dated," Livermore stressed, shoving her statement into his 'in' tray. "He's still a suspect, so I want you to go out on another date with him."

"Why are you so determined to pursue him?"

"Don't you think the fact I believe he's killed at least twice and could do so again is reason enough?"

"As you told me yourself, Chief Inspector, you've broken every rule in the book by letting me get involved in this. So I suspect there might be another reason."

Livermore gave one of his sighs. This shrewd young woman was not going to be as easily fobbed off as Buster Bates had been.

"OK. If you must know, I'm riddled with guilt. It was Jesse Singleton's mother Constance who smudged the fingerprints on the coffee mug at the crime scene by picking it up, and she then put a sofa cover over her daughter's body. Constance demanded to know why Remington wasn't being charged, and I stupidly told the poor woman she'd contaminated the evidence. I tried to make amends and give her some comfort by assuring her I'd do everything in my power to bring the killer to justice. I believe that Justin Remington is that man. That's why I want you to continue to see him."

"And if I do?"

"If you do . . .," said the chief inspector, softening his tone and leaning back in his chair, "I'm prepared to overlook that your fingerprints were in the car in which Protheroe was killed. So unless further evidence unexpectedly comes to light, it will simply go down as an unsolved crime. Protheroe was scum. The fact that he was a serial rapist means he was almost certainly the man who assaulted your sister in the same car park in which he was murdered. If you did kill him, you did every woman in the town a favour."

Katrina smiled, obviously relieved.

"But," Livermore warned, "I won't stand for any more acts of vigilantism. If your name comes up in connection with any other crime, then all bets are off."

CHAPTER THIRTY-TWO

Thursday, 10 October 2013

Nottage reported back to Livermore that they were struggling to find out much about Zena Cattermole.

"The house-to-house team has so far failed to come up with anything. Even the couple who live in the flat next door didn't really know her. They were out on the night of the murder, and the only person on the same floor who heard a scream cannot be certain what time it was."

Livermore interrupted with an expletive before Nottage could continue, "Conteh has had a long chat with Miss Cattermole's mother, but she doesn't know who her daughter had been dating. They were no longer close, and the last time she'd seen her daughter was almost a month ago."

"So she's not much help. Hopefully, we'll have more luck when we check out other relatives, friends, and contacts."

"Yes, Gov. Meanwhile, we've re-questioned the couple who discovered the body. Paula and George admit having had a lot to drink and being the worse for wear, but say they didn't delay very long in phoning us. They claim that, even allowing for the time Paula needed to recover after being sick, they phoned within five or six minutes."

Livermore nodded. "I'd also like someone to question again the neighbour who saw a man call on Zena – show her the picture of the bloke we found in the flat. Ask if it could've been him she saw and not Remington."

"Will do, Gov. What I can't get out of my head is that it's surely more than pure coincidence Remington knew Miss Cattermole and both the other two victims."

"Yes," agreed Livermore. "There's a lot pointing at him, despite the apparent flaws in the timings. If he's not the murderer and just a victim of circumstance, then he must be one hell of an unlucky guy."

*****

Zena Cattermole's little red diary, contact book, and the phone numbers stored on her mobile made interesting reading.

Conteh had finally completed the task of drawing up a list of names, and now her colleagues were discussing how the interviews should be divided among them.

Nottage was finding O'Sullivan irritating because he was not showing him the usual respect afforded to a higher-ranking officer. His ambitious colleague obviously believed the recent promotion to inspector had gone to the wrong man.

"I think I should talk to the rest of the blokes whose names appear most often on the list," O'Sullivan told the DI.

"Any particular reason you're opting for the men, Mike?"

"Well, I've already spoken to two of them after being given their names by the dating agency. There are three more members Zena met from the agency, and I'm planning to see them today. Obviously, tracing the boyfriend whose semen was found on the bed sheets in Zena's flat is a priority. Her male contacts won't be keen to admit it was theirs, and I think my Irish blarney is most likely to persuade them to reveal all. We need to play to our strengths, don't we?"

Nottage showed his disapproval of his colleague's arrogant put-down with a glare but refrained from saying the words that sprang to mind – *'You odious, jumped-up prat!'* Instead, he replied, "All right, that makes sense. Once you've seen these two dating agency members, you and Dimbleby check out the guys in Miss Cattermole's address book, diary, and her mobile. Some may prove to be merely clients for whom she worked as a designer, but there could be one or two boyfriends. Conteh and I will talk to the women whose names crop up most frequently. The rest of the names who appear only once or twice can be dealt with by other members of the team."

"Great," said O'Sullivan with a smirk. "Dim and I will make a start now. There's one name that has popped up a few times in her diary – this chap called Carl, who also left a saucy message on her answerphone. He's in Paris on business today, flogging wine to the French, would you believe? But I'll arrange to see him tomorrow morning. I'm looking forward to questioning him."

*****

Livermore, having endured an expected verbal blast from Fussy Frampton when informing him that Remington had been given an alibi by the Merton sisters, called another meeting of his team shortly before 6 p.m. to fully explain the situation.

This triggered an outburst of mumblings. "Katrina Merton must be a typical dumb blonde," muttered a disgruntled Dimbleby to nobody in particular. "The silly cow and her sister have probably got the times wrong and given Remington a 'get out of jail' card."

Livermore held up his hand for silence. "Katrina claims she's sure of the timings because he dropped them off at the cinema just before the film started. It's a big setback, but we need to press on.

"We could still get a breakthrough when we receive the lab report because three dark brown hairs were found on the victim. One of the follicles was still attached, so this could provide us with a DNA match. Now, has anyone got any new leads?"

O'Sullivan, who was sitting on his desk swinging his left leg to and fro, was the first to speak. "As I've already informed you, Gov, I went to see this woman who runs the Dream Dates agency and found that five of their members had dated Zena Cattermole. I've now spoken to all of them, and they've given accounts of where they were on the night of the murder. Their alibis seem to check out.

"I'm now concentrating on the men in Zena's contact book and on her mobile. You mentioned this guy called Carl who made a couple of suggestive remarks on her answerphone. His name also appears regularly in her diary, so I'm making him a priority."

"Right," said Livermore, turning to Nottage and Conteh. "What about the door-to-door enquiries?"

It was Nottage who replied. "They've still not been very productive. We found that Zena Cattermole was at a local hairdressing saloon on the afternoon of her murder. She talked to the hairdresser about a boyfriend – unfortunately, she didn't give any clues as to his identity, except to say he was a lousy cook but a great lover."

"Just the opposite of me," remarked one of the uniforms, causing an outbreak of laughter.

Nottage continued, "The woman two doors from Zena's flat who thinks she heard a scream believes it would've been about 9 p.m. If Zena was screaming at that time, as she was being knifed in the hall, that would, of course, definitely let Remington off the hook because he was in Eastbourne seven minutes earlier. But the woman is not even certain it was a real person screaming – she says what she heard could've been from a neighbour's television or a cat screeching. As she isn't even sure it was 9 p.m., she's not really much help.

"None of the neighbours knew Zena well. A man in the same block of flats had chatted to her briefly a couple of times without discovering anything that would be useful to us. Another neighbour – an old lady in her eighties who lives in a house nearby – saw Zena with a man two weeks ago, but couldn't give PC Bullman a proper description."

The inspector glanced across at Bullman, causing the constable to speak. "The old girl is a curtain-twitcher who doesn't miss much. She often saw Miss Cattermole coming and going and remembers her being accompanied by a man on one occasion. But all she could tell me was that the bloke was tall and probably in his thirties. At first she said he had brown hair and then thought maybe it was blond."

Livermore sighed. "Has anyone got any good news?"

"I may've stumbled upon something," piped up Dimbleby. All eyes in the room focused on the often-underrated detective sergeant.

"I've been looking through the Sex Offenders Register like you asked and checking out those who were in the area on Monday night without much success. But then I thought about the point Grace had made concerning the time gap between the murders. If the killer was desperate to satisfy his sexual appetite, then it does seem strange that, after assaulting the first two women within a month of each other, he waited four months to attack his third victim."

"Perhaps it was taking him longer to get it up," muttered O'Sullivan.

When the chuckles had died down, Dimbleby continued, "More likely explanations might be that he was serving time in prison or maybe he was hospitalised. So I checked if any of these offenders had been in clink during the four months from June to October."

Dimbleby now had everyone's full attention. "One of them was banged up for three of those months. His name is Keith Lofthouse, and he was released in mid-September – just three weeks before this latest murder."

"That's very good work, Chris," acknowledged Livermore, resisting the urge to add 'You're not so dim, after all'. "But we mustn't get too excited – we don't know if he has any connection with the previous two murders."

"Well," said Dimbleby with a smile, "I've looked through his file, and he used to work as a refuse collector in Brighton."

"Sorry," Livermore replied, rubbing the stubble on his chin, clearly puzzled. "I don't see the connection."

"It's not an obvious one, Gov, but what if he collected rubbish from the Dream Dates agency office? If he'd come across their brochures or literature in a dustbin, he could've seen details about all three murder victims."

CHAPTER THIRTY-THREE

Thursday, 10 October 2013

O'Sullivan and Dimbleby arrived at Keith Lofthouse's tiny bedsit in a backstreet in Polegate shortly before 8 p.m.

The bell didn't work, so they knocked repeatedly on a shabby front door.

"Looks like he's out," said Dimbleby. "Shall we force the lock?" As he spoke, the door was finally opened, and after identifying themselves, they were allowed in.

Lofthouse, a pathetically thin, unshaven, and unkempt apology for a man, had obviously been drinking heavily. His speech was slurred, and three empty beer tins were scattered on the lounge floor near a tatty easy chair, with a fourth tin opened and resting on a pile of magazines.

"What is it you're trying to pin on me now?" asked their ageing host. "What have you buggers come to question me about?"

"Murder," answered O'Sullivan curtly. He proceeded to arrest and caution him.

This had a devastating effect on Lofthouse. He shook his head and seemed to sober up sufficiently to understand that he was in serious trouble.

*****

Lofthouse was allowed sufficient time to fully recover from his alcoholic haze at the Eastbourne Custody Centre before being questioned in the interview room. But that didn't stop him ranting.

"Don't be so bloody stupid! I'm no murderer."

"But you have a long history as a sex offender, don't you?" chided O'Sullivan. "And you threatened one of your victims with a knife, didn't you?"

"That was years ago – and I never touched her with it. I don't even own a knife any more. You bastards confiscated it from me when you put me inside, and you never gave it back. That's against the law."

"Are you trying to be funny?" demanded O'Sullivan.

"It's not hard to get another knife, is it, Keith?" asked Dimbleby in a softer tone. "Perhaps you thought you'd use it to threaten a lady called Zena Cattermole on Monday and things got out of hand."

"I don't even know a Zenda Cattomore," the man spluttered, getting the pronunciation completely wrong.

They questioned him for fifteen more minutes, during which he kept shouting, "I didn't do it!"

"So where were you on Monday night?" asked Dimbleby.

"How the fucking hell do I know? Probably drunk out of my mind. That's what I've been reduced to after being hounded repeatedly by you pigs."

"Wrong answer," said O'Sullivan.

CHAPTER THIRTY-FOUR

Thursday, 10 October 2013

Ross Yardley was beginning to feel under pressure and was sorely tempted to end his self-imposed cigarette ban. Instead, he contented himself with stuffing another piece of chewing gum into his mouth.

But the craving for nicotine was not the only reason why he was stressed.

His reports of Zena Cattermole's murder had made the front page for two successive days, and he'd probably gleaned enough information to ensure another byline in tomorrow's paper. But now he needed to come up with a new angle, and the police were revealing very little.

As he drove across Brighton, something else filled his thoughts – his date tonight with Grace Conteh.

Ross was going around to her flat mainly because he was hoping to get inside her knickers. Her admission on the phone that she'd had a schoolgirl crush on him was ironic. At school he'd been preoccupied with dating the head girl Melanie Crowshaw, a far sexier proposition, but now Grace had matured into this highly desirable woman.

'*I must make up for lost time,*' he was thinking as he turned into her road. '*She's probably a couple of sizes too big to be a model, but she scores 10 out of 10 with me!*'

The opportunist journalist also had an ulterior motive. He'd discovered that Grace was a junior member of the police team investigating the murder, and she might be able to give him a tip off about what was going on.

So, armed with a huge bunch of roses and a bottle of wine, he presented himself on her doorstep five minutes prior to the agreed time of 8.30. Before ringing the bell, he removed a piece of chewed-up gum from his mouth and threw it on the flower bed behind him.

When Grace opened the door, she confessed she'd only got home twenty minutes earlier but had already changed into a striking red dress and red high-strapped heels. She poured him a large drink of wine, put on the music centre, and left him in the lounge while busying herself in the kitchen preparing their meal.

Ross got fed up with the Michael Bublé track that was playing and walked across the room to inspect the CD stack in the corner.

As he did so, he accidentally kicked Grace's large brown handbag, which was lying on the floor next to a chair. It was partly open, and some of the contents fell out. While putting them back, Ross came across a notebook and couldn't resist flicking through the pages. He was delighted to find it contained details about the murder investigation.

Taking out his diary and a pen from his inside coat pocket, the reporter quickly copied what Grace had written. He froze as she called out, "Are you OK in there?"

"Yes, fine," replied Ross, frantically scribbling down a couple more relevant points.

A few seconds later, he heard footsteps approaching and just managed to put away his diary and pen and thrust the notebook back in the handbag before Grace poked her head around the door.

"I was just going to put on another CD when I almost tripped over your bag," he mumbled, handing it to her.

She did not appear to suspect anything as she returned his smile and offered to get him another drink.

They were soon chatting freely over a candlelit meal of prawns, beef curry, and crème brûlée – all ready-made!

Ross told her about his love of cars. "I've just bought a new one – a Mazda 3 1.6 Tamura. It's an ex-demo model and was on offer for only £9,999, partly because it's a 13-reg, and some people think thirteen is unlucky – but not me. By trading in my old car I got it for £8,000 – a real bargain."

"I don't know much about cars," Grace confessed, sipping her wine, "but it sounds great."

"Yes, the Mazda 3 is very sleek. It's bright red. I love it."

"Do you keep it in a garage?"

"No. Where I live at Barkley Mews there are parking bays at the back. So it's under cover and quite safe."

The reporter, no longer feeling the need to pump his former schoolmate for information, left her to bring up the subject of the murder investigation.

"I saw your story in the paper today. You covered the murder very well. It puts me in a rather difficult position that we're both involved in the case, so you must appreciate that I can't discuss it with you."

"I quite understand, Grace. But it's obvious that the murder was committed by the same man who stabbed those other two women earlier this year. You're dealing with a serial killer, and I bet he used the same knife."

"I really can't comment."

Ross found her expression a real giveaway. She seemed unaware that he could read her almost like he had her notebook.

They swapped their places at the dining table for the extra comfort provided by the sofa to enjoy more music and wine.

"I've drunk too much," he said, as he kissed her tenderly on the cheek.

His words had the desired effect. "Would you like to stay?" she murmured, allowing her full lips to meet his.

To his surprise, this attractive woman was taking the initiative, and he could see by the sparkle in her eyes and saucy smile that she was offering him more than a bed for the night.

Grace led Ross into the bedroom, where she slid slowly out of the slinky red dress to stand in front of him in her underwear.

He was captivated by the sight of her in a lace and mesh basque, matching panties, and suspenders. They were all brilliant white, and the appealing contrast with her lovely black skin and sexy red high heels was a big turn-on for him.

Ross felt like a moth being drawn towards a flame as she slowly undid the buttons of his shirt. He kicked off his shoes before fumbling to undo his belt and trousers. She pushed his hands aside and smoothly completed the task for him, allowing his jeans to tumble to the floor.

Excitedly, Ross pulled her to him and brushed his lips firmly against hers. It developed into an electrifying French kiss, with his tongue probing the warm sweetness of her soft mouth.

Grace, like him, seemed to be consumed by burning arousal. She groaned as his fingers caressed her neck and moved inside the top of her basque to fondle her firm breasts. He bent his head to suck one pert nipple, and then the other, before kneeling down to stroke the tops of her shapely legs, which soon became taut.

Twirling around, she removed her tiny silk panties. Ross kissed her ample bottom cheeks repeatedly, and when she eventually turned to face him, he marvelled at the fully exposed curly black forest that now confronted him.

He caught his breath and whispered, "You're truly beautiful." Then his long fingers slipped softly through her pubic hairs.

Her moans spurred him on, and spreading out his fingers, he used them to comb her.

Ross followed this erotic gesture by again using his tongue, this time to lick her most sensitive area.

"You'd better stop that or you'll make me do something you might not like," she whispered.

"And what would that be?"

"You'll make me lose control . . . and I might start to pee. I can't help myself if I'm licked down there."

"Don't worry about it – I'd love to taste every bit of you," he told her and promptly resumed licking.

Within seconds he felt a warm, wet liquid trickling on to his lips.

"Lovely," he muttered.

"Would you like some more?"

"Yes, please."

When she'd finished, they moved on to the bed. While he lay down, she sat upright, fixing him with a seductive stare and running her tongue over her lower lip. She caressed her left breast with one hand before leaning over and gently rubbing his erection with the other. Her tender touch soon caused his penis to reach maximum height and thickness.

Grace then slid on top of him and guided the rock-hard weapon towards her extremely wet crevice.

Once he was deep inside her, she cried out, "Fuck me. Fuck me hard!"

He did as she requested, though he could hardly do otherwise because her left hand was pulling him backwards and forwards by his balls. He came within seconds, but she continued to use him as a dildo until she finally shouted, "YES, YES, YES!"

*****

As they lay on the bed spent, Ross couldn't suppress a big smile.

'What a lucky bastard I am! Who would've guessed that this seemingly demure policewoman would turn out to be such a vamp in bed? I wonder if she wears sexy underwear even when she's in uniform!'

He turned towards the naked body next to him and stroked one of Grace's gorgeous breasts. The large nipple immediately became hard.

'WOW! She's ready for more! She's not only proving the best lay I've ever had, but she's also provided me with vital information about the murder. I just hope she doesn't realise I've been through her notebook – if she does, she'll have my balls again!'

CHAPTER THIRTY-FIVE

Friday, 11 October 2013

Ross and Grace enjoyed a repeat performance the next morning which caused her to use the 'F' word again. But this time it was in annoyance because she suddenly realised she was going to be late for work.

To make matters worse, her normally reliable Honda wouldn't start. Ross quickly inspected it, pronounced that there was a fault with her starter motor, and offered to give her a lift.

Grace hurriedly left the key under one of the wheels of the faithful old rust bucket after phoning her friendly mechanic to come and repair it. Then she quickly slid into the passenger seat of Ross's new pride and joy.

Despite Ross's daredevil driving, which blatantly exceeded the speed limit, she was still late when he dropped her off at the police HQ.

The concerned constable could see Nottage impatiently pacing up and down in the car park as she alighted from the bright red Mazda.

"That's the reporter who used to go to school with you, isn't it?" asked her clearly miffed colleague when she walked up to him.

"Yes."

"So you two are going out together."

"I've only seen him a couple of times."

"And by the looks of it, he spent the night with you. Reporters are the last blokes you should be sleeping with," Nottage admonished as she got into his car.

"Who said anything about sleeping with him?"

"Come off it, Grace. I don't have to be a detective to work out how he happened to be giving you a lift this early in the morning. And you're blushing, which is a dead giveaway."

Conteh's right hand automatically went to her cheek to try to hide her embarrassment, but the unsympathetic Nottage continued rebuking her. "I hope you haven't discussed the case with him."

"Of course not."

"The situation wouldn't be so bad if it wasn't for the fact he's covering the murder. I've seen his name on a story in this morning's paper. Ross . . ."

"Yardley. He's a freelance, so he writes for more than one paper."

"That's even worse," Nottage said, taking a turning too sharply. "Did Mr Yardley ask you anything about the injuries to the victims when you were in bed together last night?"

"It didn't come up."

"Didn't it?" he smirked, obviously choosing to interpret her choice of phrase in a smutty context. "It would have done if I'd been with you. But there's nothing wrong with Mr Yardley's news sense. And if he prints anything that Livermore said we mustn't reveal, then I wouldn't like to be in your shoes."

'No, but you'd obviously like to be in my pants.' She was tempted to tell him so but, instead, talked about the task ahead. "Let's hope we're going to have better luck with our door knocking today than we did yesterday. The five women we've already seen have told us next to nothing. All we've learned is that Zena did design work for a couple of them over a year ago, and another only vaguely remembered meeting her."

During the next ninety minutes they visited the homes of four more women whose names were in Zena's contact book or listed on her mobile.

Two of them offered little worthwhile information, apart from raving about her ability as a designer to combine colours, furnishings, and fabrics that matched their lifestyles. The other two women were out.

"This is really pissing me off," complained Nottage. "I actually phoned this friend of Zena's called Gloria Bradshaw and told her we'd be coming. So there's no excuse for her not being at home. How could it slip her memory?"

"I bet she wanted to avoid seeing us. Probably thinks she's being clever by going out."

"Well, she won't feel so bloody clever when I haul her into the station."

The previous day they'd been to the office of Zena's brother Laurie and found that he was away on a business trip until the end of the week.

"Why don't we try the brother's home?" Conteh suggested. "His wife might know something."

At first it seemed that their call on Zena's sister-in-law Rita was going to be another waste of time. The woman, a thirtyish, slightly overweight redhead who announced she was about to dash off to the hairdressers, said they would need to come back and talk to Laurie when he returned the next day.

"We weren't very close to Zena, but we were horrified to hear about her being killed like that," blurted out Rita, struggling into her coat. "Do you know when the funeral is? Laurie and I will go, of course. And I expect a lot of the girls from the club will want to turn up for it too."

"What club would that be?" asked Nottage.

"The Krazy Knights."

"The nightclub? Was Zena a member?"

"No – she worked there."

"We thought she was an interior designer."

"That's what she told her mother," laughed Rita. "She did a lot of designing at one stage and perhaps still dabbled in it, but Zena had been doing lap dancing and pole dancing for over a year. Why don't you talk to her friends Gloria Bradshaw and Pixie Whitechurch? They worked at the Krazy Knights club with her."

"We've been around to Gloria's flat, but she was out," said Conteh. "Pixie will be our next port of call. Do you happen to know anything about the men Zena was seeing?"

"No. The last time Laurie and I spoke to her was on the phone about three weeks ago, and she didn't mention anyone. But Pixie should be able to tell you. Sorry – I must go or I'll be late."

With that Rita slammed her front door behind her and marched towards her parked car.

As she got into her yellow Honda Civic, a much newer model than Conteh's, she called over her shoulder to them, "At the club, Zena was known as Anna Marie."

*****

Nottage immediately phoned Livermore to bring him up to date. "Gov, there's been a new development, I think, will interest you."

"Well, I hope it's more useful than the one that O'Sullivan and Dimbleby came up with. They brought in this sex offender, Keith Lofthouse, and thought they'd found our killer until CCTV footage in his local off-licence in Polegate showed that he was miles from the crime scene on Monday night. I've just been watching a tape of the idiot staggering into the store in a drunken stupor trying to buy some more booze. Even if there'd been enough time for him to get to Brighton, he wouldn't have been in a fit state to do so, and certainly not cut someone's throat."

"I've got some more helpful news, Gov."

"And what would that be?

"Four of the women we've spoken to confirmed Zena Cattermole did work as an interior designer, but it turns out that she switched to a more risqué profession as a nightclub lap dancer."

"Are you sure?"

"That's what her sister-in-law tells us. Obviously we'll check it out."

"Why on earth would a stripper want to be a member of a dating agency? She would hardly have been short of admirers, would she?"

"It's rather odd, isn't it?" Nottage agreed. "But she'd worked for a year as a dancer at the Krazy Knights."

"We've had our eyes on that place, haven't we?"

"Yes, Gov. Some of their 'artistes' are known to give clients sex for cash."

"So Zena may have been little more than a high-class hooker," Livermore observed. "That would explain why she'd so many sex toys in her flat. And it opens up a new line of enquiry."

"She was apparently leading a double life, Gov. To a lot of people, including her mother, she was a designer. They had no idea she also had other talents performing pole and lap dancing. At the Krazy Knights, she didn't work under her own name. She was known at the club as Anna Marie."

Nottage paused while the DCI gave one of his frequent sighs. Then he put into words what Livermore was loathe to admit. "We can no longer assume that the murderer must have come into contact with his three victims through the dating agency. We now have to consider the possibility that he may've met Zena, or rather her alter ego Anna Marie, at the night club. So we could have a load more suspects."

CHAPTER THIRTY-SIX

Friday, 11 October 2013

Pixie Whitechurch, a voluptuous peroxide blonde, was not only at home, but her laid-back demeanour suggested she had plenty of time to talk.

Conteh introduced herself and Nottage. As Pixie leaned forward to hold out her hand to shake his, her ample bosoms almost tumbled out of her loose-fitting short top that also revealed her bare midriff, where a silver ring was embedded in her navel.

"Good grief!" Nottage was about to exclaim in disapproval but stopped himself in mid-sentence and changed it to "Good . . . to meet you." Unfortunately, his stare and open mouth gave him away.

"Cheeky!" Pixie rebuked him.

Nottage's face was almost as red as the curtains in the brightly coloured lounge of Pixie's flat, which was situated in one of Brighton's many side streets.

"I'm devastated about Zena being killed," the self-assured woman told them. "She was a good friend, and we also worked together."

"As lap dancers at the Krazy Knights nightclub?" checked Nottage.

"Yes," said Pixie, sitting down on a stool and crossing one long leg over the other so swiftly that the policeman thought her pink skintight jeans might split, "we did lap dancing and pole dancing."

"And she was known by clients as Anna Marie?"

"That's right."

"And just what did her work involve?"

"Didn't your mother ever tell you about nightclubs? You ought to get out more, darling."

Nottage was grateful that Conteh came to his aid. "What my colleague and I want to know is whether Zena gave clients any 'extras'?"

"What do you take us for?" hissed Pixie indignantly. "We're paid to entertain clients by dancing for them, either on poles or at their tables. There's no sex involved."

"Come off it," scoffed Nottage. "You don't expect me to believe that, do you?"

"You can believe what you like, darling," Pixie retorted, pushing a wayward strand of her dyed hair back into place.

"Look, Pixie," said Conteh in a friendly voice, "we're not here to pass judgement on you or look into what money you may've earned on the side. This is a murder investigation, and we need to find the killer before he strikes again. So please tell us about anyone Zena had sex with."

Pixie, having lit a cigarette, blew out a puff of smoke while she appeared to consider the implications. "OK, I'll tell you. But first I want to make it clear that not all the dancers do 'extras'. We're not prostitutes."

Conteh nodded.

"Like me and the other girls, Zena was paid by the club simply to entertain clients on the premises. It's up to us if we want to go with them and have sex afterwards. Some girls do and some girls don't. One of them, Penny, has such a high opinion of herself that I'd be surprised if the stuck-up cow's had sex with anyone. But my friend Tootsie can't get enough of it. Just like office girls or shop assistants, we're all different. As far as I know, only three of us, including Zena, provided a special sexual service."

"Presumably the clients arranged this with you girls direct and paid you in cash," Nottage pressed.

"Of course. But, as I say, only some girls do that, and not with just anyone. Zena would only accept payment for 'extras' if she took a liking to one of the clients."

"Can you tell us the names of the guys she went with?"

"I only know about three or four, and that's just by their first names. There was a 'Maurice' and a 'Vernon', who I also went with, and a bit of an oddball, Zena mentioned, called Rick. More recently, there was a rather kinky guy named Boris."

"In what way was Boris kinky?" Nottage wanted to know.

Pixie inhaled before telling him, "He wanted Zena to do a role play and impersonate his girlfriend. She told me about it, and we had a good laugh. Boris – if that was his real name – got Zena to act as if she was this frigid woman who had to be coaxed into even lifting her skirt. His sexual fantasy was to seduce her into taking down her panties, rubbing his cock, and sucking him off. He knew exactly what he wanted and had explained to Zena that she must act shy and innocent. He was articulate and well-spoken – not like some of the berks who are tongue-tied or just call us names."

"Anything else you can think of?"

"Not much. Zena went along with it because Boris was also good-looking and paid very well. Some club members can be quite generous with tips, and a few offer to pay a lot in 'extras', but Boris gave Zena more than the norm. What I'd give for a client like that."

"Do you know how we might be able to find this Boris?"

"I'm afraid I wouldn't, darling. The nightclub should be able to tell you. If you go there, ask for Denton. But he only knew Zena as Anna Marie."

"One more thing," said Nottage, trying to take his eyes off Pixie's boobs but only succeeding in staring at another part of her soft pink flesh near where the silver navel ring was placed. "Did you know that Zena was also a member of the Dream Dates and Friendships dating agency?"

"Yes, she mentioned it."

"Is that a cover for an escort agency?"

"No, darling, I don't think so. As far as I know, it's just a dating agency for professional men and women. Zena thought it would be a good idea to go out with a few of their clients and then offer them sex for cash or encourage them to buy her expensive presents. She was a greedy, unscrupulous little madam."

Conteh was quick to pick up on this. "But what was the point of her joining an ordinary dating agency instead of an escort agency? Surely it's unusual for a nightclub dancer to do that?"

"I suppose it is, but Zena saw it as another string to her bow. She was fussy who she had sex with. At the nightclub, we have to perform for whoever comes in, irrespective of what they look like, but at the dating agency, she was shown pictures of the men first so she could pick and choose."

"Was that how she first met Boris?"

"No. She told me the first time she saw him was when he came into Krazy Knights. He asked her to lap dance for him and then persuaded her to provide some 'extras'."

"When Zena talked about Boris asking her to pretend to be his girlfriend, did she mention what the girlfriend was called?"

"Yeah. His little Miss Innocent was named Suzie."

'Blimey!' thought Nottage. 'Conteh is on the ball with her questioning.' It prompted him to ask, "Do you know where Zena acted out Boris's sexual fantasy?"

"Usually she'd go with a client to a hotel room, but I think in his case she took him to her apartment. He passed Zena's three main requirements – he was dishy, interesting, and loaded with money!"

CHAPTER THIRTY-SEVEN

Friday, 11 October 2013

The next stop for Nottage and Conteh was the Krazy Knights nightclub in a seedy part of Brighton. The club was on a corner, and one street was lined with black rubbish bags, clustered around overfilled wheelie bins.

The officers were taken down a poorly lit corridor to an office where they had the dubious pleasure of meeting the club's swarthy owner Denton Doyle.

Nottage took an instant dislike to the uncooperative, moon-faced man in a tight-fitting dark blue suit that did his ample frame no favours.

"Sorry, there's not a lot I can tell you," Doyle said flatly when they talked in his stuffy office, which seemed to double as a storeroom because it contained several cardboard boxes as well as a large desk, two filing cabinets, and a dying pot plant.

He was even less forthcoming about clients Anna Marie had gone with. "She worked here for about a year and was popular with the members, but whether she went out with any of them I wouldn't know." He spoke in a deep, throaty rasp that suggested he was a heavy smoker, as was confirmed by the nicotine stains on his fingers.

"Don't insult our intelligence," Nottage rebuked. "Obviously, you're fully aware that she and some of your other girls had sex with club members."

"If you think I'm going to admit that, then you're insulting MY intelligence, Officer," Doyle retorted, brushing a couple of flecks of dandruff from his shoulder.

"OK, just give us the names and addresses of all your members," said Nottage.

"I'm not prepared to do that – my members are entitled to their privacy," the charmless man insisted, taking out a cigarette packet from his pocket and lighting up. He seemed incapable of keeping still.

"You're not being very helpful," Nottage told him. Using a different tactic, he added, "I'm sure you don't want to obstruct a murder investigation, sir. It's the duty of every upright member of the community to cooperate in such serious matters."

Doyle was not swayed. "Sorry," he repeated, drawing on his cigarette. "It's a matter of client confidentially. I'm sure you understand."

"You're facing a moral dilemma," said Conteh, smiling at him.

Nottage noted that this slight show of affability caused the recalcitrant oaf to ogle the police constable's shapely legs before making eye contact with her.

Conteh carried on speaking. "Unfortunately, if we can't find out what we want from you, we will have to go through other channels such as officials at Her Majesty's Revenue and Customs. But that might alert them to any payments received by you or your girls which have not been declared."

"I'm not responsible for what my dancers do about their tax returns," sneered Doyle, blowing out a waft of cigarette smoke towards the police officers.

"Maybe, maybe not," said Conteh. "But if you or your girls are investigated for tax evasion and VAT irregularities, then it could be far-reaching."

"That's right," added Nottage, following the lead of his quick-thinking junior officer. "Furthermore, we might have to send uniformed officers to the club to check members' identities for ourselves by standing on the door."

Doyle sighed, stubbed out his cigarette, and got up to rummage in a battered filing cabinet draw.

A few minutes later, Nottage and Conteh left Krazy Knights with a complete list of clients' names, addresses, and phone numbers.

They were particularly interested in one called Boris.

CHAPTER THIRTY-EIGHT

Friday, 11 October 2013

O'Sullivan felt they had struck gold – literally – when he and Dimbleby called on the man whose name kept cropping up in Zena Cattermole's diary and address book.

As they approached Carl Tarbutt's large detached house, the gravel on his winding drive scrunched beneath the tyres of their car. They parked beside a shining gold Italian sports two-seater.

"He must be loaded," O'Sullivan said, using the gold knocker on the oak-panelled front door, which was opened within seconds by a man whose love of gold was obvious.

O'Sullivan took in the expensive casual shirt and sweater, medallion, large ring, and capped tooth behind thick lips. All were gold.

"Are you Carl Tarbutt?"

"I am. And who might you two chancers be?"

The policemen showed their warrant cards and gave their names, before O'Sullivan continued, "We're making enquiries concerning the death of a Miss Zena Cattermole, and we'd like to ask you a few questions."

"You'd better come in then."

O'Sullivan saw further proof of Tarbutt's wealth in tasteful furnishings, Persian carpets, and ornate mirrors as the assertive wheeler-dealer showed the policemen into his study and firmly shut the door.

"Yes, I knew Zena Cattermole, and I was very upset to read about her death."

"How well did you know her?"

"We were friends."

"Can you expand on that, sir?" O'Sullivan said, clearly not satisfied with the vague answer the man had provided. "We know from her diary and her telephone records that you spoke to her quite often. And she had a picture of you in a frame in her flat. That suggests you were more than just friends, doesn't it?"

"We went out a few times," Tarbutt responded.

"When did you first meet her, sir?"

"Oh, about two years ago. We met at a party, and she told me she was an interior designer. I asked her advice when I bought this place and wanted to redecorate it. She also came up with some design suggestions for a block of flats I purchased to rent out."

"Shall we cut to the chase?" Dimbleby said bluntly. "Were you having a sexual relationship with her?"

"I'm a happily married man."

O'Sullivan decided to play hardball. "Sir, this is a murder enquiry, and we need to know what sort of relationship you were having with Miss Cattermole. You can either tell us now and we can be discreet or we can make enquiries of our own."

"Very well, Sergeant. We did have a sexual relationship."

"Where would the sex have taken place?"

"At her flat."

"Would that have been in the bedroom, sir?"

At that moment, the study door opened. O'Sullivan paused from writing notes on his pad and watched as an attractive woman in her early thirties – probably a little younger than Tarbutt – entered. "Sorry to interrupt you," she said. "I'm just going out, darling, and need some cash."

"OK, angel," Tarbutt replied, taking a wad of notes from his trouser pocket and thrusting half of them into her hand. He made no attempt to introduce the two policemen, but the well-dressed brunette acknowledged them.

"Hi, I'm Carl's wife."

They nodded and smiled without telling her who they were.

"These gentlemen are here on business," Tarbutt explained.

"Please don't tell me you're selling Carl anything made of gold. We don't need any more."

"Nothing like that," Dimbleby volunteered. "I can see you've already got more gold in this house than they have in Fort Knox."

Mrs Tarbutt grimaced, kissed her husband on the cheek, and was gone.

O'Sullivan wasted no time in continuing his questioning. "Was it in her bedroom that you had sex with Miss Cattermole?" he repeated.

"Yes, it was. Is that really significant?"

"We found traces of semen in the bedroom," O'Sullivan explained. "Would you be willing to provide a DNA sample? It simply means us taking a swab of your saliva from inside your mouth."

"If you think it's necessary, Officer."

"Good. And when was the last time you saw her?"

"That would've been last week – I called in to see her at her flat on Friday."

"Did you have sex with her in her bedroom on Friday?"

"Yes."

"And you left her a message on her answerphone on Sunday. Did she phone you back?"

"No, but I'm sure she would've done. We had agreed to meet up early next week."

"And where were you on Monday night?" chipped in Dimbleby.

"At home most of the time."

"Can your wife vouch for that?"

"Yes, she can, but I'd rather not bring her into this. I admit I didn't get home until almost 10 p.m., as I'd been driving back from a business trip to Coventry."

"Presumably your wife didn't know about your relationship with Miss Cattermole," Dimbleby assumed.

"No. It's not the sort of thing you boast about to your wife, is it?"

"Was Miss Cattermole aware that you were married?" Dimbleby put to the clearly agitated businessman.

"Yes, she was. So if you think I had some sort of motive for killing Zena, you're very much mistaken."

"On the contrary, sir," Dimbleby came back. "If Miss Cattermole was threatening to tell your wife about your adulterous sexual liaisons, then you had a very good motive indeed."

CHAPTER THIRTY-NINE

Friday, 11 October 2013

When Nottage and Conteh returned to Livermore's office, they found O'Sullivan already in there, sitting talking to the chief inspector.

"So," O'Sullivan was saying, "most of the men Dimbleby and I interviewed whose names appeared in Zena Cattermole's address book were either her old interior design clients or casual acquaintances. And they had alibis for the night she was murdered. But Carl Tarbutt was having an affair with her – and he cannot prove where he was for part of that evening. So I'll be making some enquiries and then speak to him again. At first he wasn't keen to volunteer any details of his relationship with Zena, but a little gentle persuasion worked wonders, and he finally admitted having sex with her three days before she was killed. He's given a DNA sample, and I believe we'll find it was his semen on the bed sheets in her flat."

"So you think Carl Tarbutt is a real suspect?" Livermore asked, after waving Nottage and Conteh to come in.

"It all depends if he can prove he wasn't in Brighton on Monday night," the sergeant replied. "If he was driving back from Coventry in his flash gold car, as he claims, then there should be something on one of the motorway cameras. But he probably had time to get to Brighton. He certainly fits the bill. He's married, and his wife didn't know about his affair with Zena. Carl's main concern is that she does not find out. If Zena was threatening to tell his wife, then he had a motive. But there's nothing to link him to the other two murder victims. In fact, he was abroad on holiday when one of them was killed."

Livermore sighed. "We seem to be doing a better job of eliminating likely candidates than we do of building up a case against them."

"But Tarbutt was a font of useful information, Gov," O'Sullivan quickly added. "He revealed that, in addition to being an interior designer, Zena was a lap dancer at the Krazy Knights nightclub."

"Yes, so Nottage and Conteh found out earlier," Livermore confirmed. He looked across at them and enquired, "Did you two come up with anything?"

"We've obtained a list of clients from the Krazy Knights," Nottage told him. "We haven't followed up on them yet, but one is a solicitor who is known to us. He's worked on criminal cases as well as dealing with the administration of estates. He even did some conveyancing for a friend of mine."

"Well, I haven't got time for tittle-tattle," scoffed O'Sullivan, smirking as he got to his feet.

"I'm not referring to this solicitor as idle gossip, Michael," Nottage corrected his colleague. "He could be our murderer. His name is Boris Kimble, and we've discovered that while Zena was working at the club, under the alias 'Anna Marie', she provided 'extras' for a man called Boris. She told one of her fellow dancers how he got her to act out a kinky sexual fantasy. Perhaps he wanted a repeat performance, and it all went wrong."

CHAPTER FORTY

Friday, 11 October 2013

Nottage and Conteh were duly dispatched to interview Boris Kimble at the Brighton offices of solicitors Caughton, McGerity, and Yates.

On the way, Nottage confided to his colleague that O'Sullivan was getting up his nose.

"What he said about 'tittle-tattle' was rather crass," Conteh agreed. "Do you think he's trying to undermine you?"

"Too right, I do. He clearly can't stand me being promoted to DI and him being overlooked."

"I suppose O'Sullivan's jealous of the fact that DCI Livermore has so much confidence in you," Conteh suggested. "Perhaps it's a big bone of contention with him."

"Look, I shouldn't be having this conversation with you, Grace."

"Sorry, Jeff, if I overstepped the mark."

"No, it's my fault. I shouldn't be talking to you about another officer. But what we say in the car stays in the car, right?"

"Of course," she assured him.

"I'm glad to hear that you feel the chief is supportive of me. But perhaps he's too much so – not just supportive but even protective."

"Sorry, I don't understand, Jeff."

"This is my first murder case as a DI, and I feel the chief wants to cover my backside. He's very 'hands on' anyway, but I feel he's taking too much of a lead role in this case instead of letting me run the show. Maybe that's part of the reason why O'Sullivan doesn't fully respect me."

Conteh was embarrassed that her senior officer had confided so much in her but felt she should point out something that Nottage wasn't fully grasping.

"I think the reason the chief has got so involved is that it's become a personal issue with him – he's determined to nail Justin Remington. The chief was livid when the CPS wouldn't allow him to charge Remington with the first two murders because he was convinced he'd committed them."

"You've got a good point there," Nottage acknowledged. "And it strikes me as strange that the chief isn't concerned about the apparent connection with Katrina Merton. My hunch is that her fingerprints are among those in the car in which that rapist Protheroe was shot, and now she's going out with a murder suspect. She's even given him an alibi. I just hope the chief isn't being taken in by her looks and charms."

"Come off it, Jeff. Livermore's hardly a lady's man."

"All I'm saying is that he could end up with egg on his face."

"Do you think that's likely?"

"It would certainly be the case if Katrina has committed some offence. And it would be really bad for the chief if it emerges that she killed Protheroe in revenge for him raping her sister."

Conteh's mobile phone pinged. She checked it and saw a text message from Ross. It read, 'You were sex-sational.'

*****

The glass-fronted premises of Caughton, McGerity, and Yates housed a large reception area in which the police seated themselves on a brown leather sofa while they waited for Kimble to finish seeing a client.

Conteh flicked through the fashion magazine she'd picked up from the coffee table in front of her, while Nottage wrote in his notebook a couple of questions that he needed to ask the solicitor.

As someone walked past to leave the building, the svelte female receptionist called out to them, "Mr Kimble can see you now."

They were invited to sit on comfortable high-backed chairs in a plush office, where the plain white walls were decorated with three small pictures of local landmarks.

When they informed Kimble that they wanted to question him in relation to a murder, he joked, "Do I need a solicitor present?" The police officers did not laugh.

"Presumably you've read about the murder of Zena Cattermole in Brighton?" asked Nottage.

"Yes," said Boris from behind his large glass-topped desk. "It's quite horrific."

"She was killed on Monday night," Nottage continued. "Can you account for your movements on Monday night, sir?"

"Yes, I can if I have to, but I don't see why I should."

"We believe you knew her, sir."

"No, I didn't. I'd remember if she was a client of mine."

"It was the other way around, sir. We believe you were a client of hers."

"Sorry, I don't understand," Boris replied pompously, flicking a small fleck of dust off the lapel of his immaculate pinstriped suit in a movement Nottage found was reminiscent of Denton Doyle.

The policeman got to the point. "Zena Cattermole was a dancer at the Krazy Knights nightclub at which you're a member."

"Yes, I'm a member there, but I don't know a dancer called Zena."

"She worked under the name of Anna Marie," Nottage explained.

"Anna Marie," repeated Boris in a tone that seemed to imply a mixture of recognition and shock, but he remained adamant. "She may have been one of the pole dancers, but I don't recall meeting any Anna Marie."

"Her specialty was lap dancing for some of the punters," said Conteh. "And she gave certain clients sexual favours."

"I don't go with prostitutes."

"Well, you appear to have gone with this one, sir," replied the policewoman politely but firmly. "She acted out a sexual fantasy for a man of your name."

"It wasn't me."

Nottage wasn't convinced. "So how do you explain the fact that Anna Marie told her friend she performed a sexual role play with a man called Boris, and you're the only 'Boris' on the Krazy Knights' membership list?"

"Perhaps some bloke gave a false name and happened to pick mine."

"And just why would they come up with your name, sir?" asked Conteh in a calm, measured tone.

"I don't know, young lady. But that's the only explanation I can think of – I've already told you it wasn't me."

Nottage didn't buy into Boris's denials, and he hated to be outsmarted. *'Two can play at games,'* he thought, remembering that Pixie had said the man calling himself Boris had asked Anna Marie to pretend she was his girlfriend Suzie.

One 'Suzie' immediately came to Nottage's mind – Suzie Merton. Surely that was too much of a stretch, but it was worth taking a punt.

"Is Suzie Merton a client of yours, Mr Kimble?"

Boris hesitated, seemingly caught off guard. "I have represented her. I did the conveyancing when she obtained her flat in a part-buy/part-rent scheme."

"No doubt you also advised her after she was assaulted in a car park last year."

"Yes, I did, but I don't see what that has to do with your murder investigation, Inspector."

"Maybe nothing at all," Nottage acknowledged, trying to think how he could unnerve this clever solicitor. "It's just interesting that you know Suzie Merton so well."

The solicitor's face reddened, but he remained silent.

"You see, the man calling himself 'Boris' to Anna Marie asked her to impersonate his girlfriend – a lady called Suzie."

CHAPTER FORTY-ONE

Friday, 11 October 2013

Back at the police station, Nottage told Livermore what he and Conteh had discovered about Boris Kimble.

"He's the only 'Boris' on the Krazy Knights' membership list, so we didn't believe him when he denied having met Zena Cattermole. It seems pretty obvious to us that he knew her as Anna Marie. He must've been the guy called Boris for whom she acted out a sexual fantasy, pretending to be his girlfriend Suzie. I'd bet any money you like that he was referring to Suzie Merton."

"What makes you say that?"

"He admits that Suzie Merton is a client of his – so it makes sense that she was the girlfriend referred to on the tape as 'Suzie'. We'll make further checks, of course, but he can't be ruled out as a suspect, Gov."

"What are you suggesting, Jeff?"

"I'm beginning to think Grace's theory is correct, and there could be two different murderers. Maybe the first two women were victims of a psycho, but Zena was killed by Boris Kimble."

"What was his motive?"

"My original thought was that he wanted Zena to act out another sexual fantasy and she refused. But there's an alternative scenario – perhaps Zena started to blackmail him. Boris had paid to have sex with her, and maybe she was threatening to spill the beans to his girlfriend."

"It's an interesting theory, Jeff, but we mustn't jump to conclusions. Even if you're right, we'll need to be absolutely sure of our facts because Kimble is one tricky customer in court. He's so good he could get Stevie Wonder off a driving offence!"

"But it makes sense, Gov. It would explain why the first two women were knifed in the heart, while Zena had her throat cut. Two different methods – two different killers."

Livermore nodded thoughtfully. "If that's the case, then it could not only make Boris Kimble a suspect for this latest murder, but Zena's boyfriend Carl Tarbutt as well."

*****

That night Grace received two more saucy texts from Ross. The first called her 'the best lay of my life', and the second asked, 'Are you into telephone sex?'

When her phone rang immediately afterwards, she answered it and heard heavy breathing. "Go on, then. Talk dirty to me," she said.

"I don't think that would be appropriate," wheezed her asthmatic father.

"Sorry, Dad. I thought it was someone else."

"I hope you did – I'd hate to think that's what you say to everyone who phones you."

"Only those with heavy breathing."

"Yes, well, my asthma is no better despite the wonderful climate here in Senegal. But it's your mother I'm ringing about – she's been taken ill."

"What's the matter with her – is it very serious?"

"Yes. She's been admitted to a hospital in Dakar, and they've diagnosed that a kidney infection has caused blood poisoning."

"Is that life-threatening?"

"It can be. The hospital say they hope they can treat her successfully, but her age is against her. I was wondering if you can fly out to Senegal to be with us."

There was a long silence while Grace contemplated how she could possibly drop everything and travel 2,700 miles to Dakar.

"Grace, are you still there?"

"Yes, of course, I'll try to come, Dad, but I might not be able to do so right away. I'm in the middle of a murder investigation. Let me talk to my boss about it tomorrow and get back to you."

CHAPTER FORTY-TWO

Saturday, 12 October 2013

The persistent ringing of the phone put paid to any chance Grace had of a Saturday morning lie-in.

"Hello," she muttered into the mouthpiece, still not fully awake.

"You idiot!" shouted the voice at the other end. It was Nottage.

"Nice to hear your friendly voice, Inspector."

"You absolute idiot!"

"Why? What have I done?"

"You've given your boyfriend the very facts we wanted to withhold. That's what you've bloody well done."

"No, I haven't."

"So how do you explain the story in this morning's paper headlined, 'SERIAL KILLER COULD STRIKE AGAIN' with Yardley's byline on it? It refers to the killer cutting all three women under the chin and what type of knife he used. Livermore will go stark raving bloody mad when he reads this. It's the very thing he told us all to keep quiet. He may even take you off the case. I've got a lot of time for you, Grace, and I think you've the makings of a first-class police officer, but you've made a big error of judgement over this."

"I swear I didn't tell Ross anything."

"Perhaps you talk in your sleep?" Nottage suggested, his tone full of sarcasm. "You're a bloody fool going to bed with him."

"I didn't give Ross those details. I certainly didn't tell him anything about the victims being cut first. The case was only mentioned very briefly, and it was Ross who told me that he believed a serial killer was using the same knife. I don't know how he got his information." Then suddenly the penny dropped. "Oh my God! My handbag! He picked it up off the floor. He must've taken out my notebook and read it."

"While you were lying in bed, no doubt."

"No, while I was cooking the dinner. The bastard has stitched me up."

In view of the dressing-down Nottage had given her, Grace decided against asking him about taking time off to go to Senegal. Instead, she phoned her father to say that she was unable to fly out immediately, but if her mother did not improve, she would do her utmost to visit her later in the week.

CHAPTER FORTY-THREE

Saturday, 12 October 2013

Suzie cursed the fact she'd broken one of the lenses in her glasses. She needed them when reading smaller type and so promptly made an appointment at the optician's in Eastbourne town centre for Saturday morning.

She was disappointed to learn that her normal optician, dear old Mr Oakley, had retired, but was surprised to discover she knew his replacement. It was Justin Remington, her sister's friend who'd given them a lift to the cinema.

The strange thing was he didn't appear to recognise her.

"Don't you remember me?" she asked. "My sister Katrina introduced us."

"Oh yes, of course," he mumbled.

After the minimum of conversation, Remington told Suzie to look into an upright instrument consisting of a microscope, lens, and light. She placed her chin on the rest and peered into the machine, one eye at a time. The optician, viewing from the other side of the slit-lamp biomicroscope, instructed Suzie to focus on his ear so he could look at her iris, cornea, and retina through the lens.

"Have you taken over from Mr Oakley?" she asked.

"Yes. He retired earlier this year. Now please keep your head still, Miss Merton. Just look at my ear."

She did as instructed and noticed that his right ear had a scar on it. The blemish was shaped like a 'U' with the ends curving inwards, similar to a horseshoe.

Within minutes Suzie was prescribed as needing +2 lenses, which could easily be fitted in her existing frames. They would be ready to collect in three days' time.

Being without glasses was going to be a nuisance, but her mind dwelt on the fact that the optician hadn't recognised her.

So much for Boris telling her how attractive she was – this man couldn't even remember her!

CHAPTER FORTY-FOUR

Saturday, 12 October, 2013

Grace Conteh was furious when she read Ross's story. It gave chapter and verse about the facts contained in her notebook. She would make him pay for his act of betrayal. But how? Then it came to her.

His pride and joy was his new Mazda Tamura. He'd told her that he left it parked behind his flat in Barkley Mews. A bright red 13-reg shouldn't be hard to spot.

It was only 9.35 a.m., and, with any luck, Ross would still be at home, so his car would be in its parking bay.

Stopping only to make a purchase from a hardware shop, she drove around to Barkley Mews.

Grace had no difficulty in spotting the shiny Mazda Tamura in one of the covered parking bays. She parked her own newly repaired Honda on the adjoining side road and sat in it, waiting for Ross to come out of his flat. After forty minutes he emerged.

As he walked towards his car, she ran up to him, shouting, "You bastard. You went through my handbag and read my notebook, didn't you?"

"It was an accident. I tripped over your bag and the contents fell out on to the floor. I didn't . . ."

He was cut short by a stinging slap across the face that knocked the piece of gum he'd been chewing on to the ground.

But Grace was not finished. She turned sharply, strode up to his precious car, and squirted some liquid from the can she was holding on to the bonnet.

"What have you done?" he gasped, rubbing the cheek that had been hit so fiercely.

"I've given it an acid finish," she said, watching with satisfaction as the paintwork blistered. "You were quite wrong to think a 13-reg wouldn't be unlucky."

Grace drove home with a smug expression on her face. But there was something else eating away at her – a nagging notion at the back of her mind that she was trying desperately to recall.

If only she could remember. *'Ah!'* she thought at last. *'There was something odd about the way Pixie Whitechurch had spoken of Zena's sex session with Boris.'*

On a whim, she did a detour and headed for Pixie's flat.

"Oh, it's you again," said the blonde nightclub dancer. "You're lucky to catch me in – I'm just about to leave for a lunch date before I go to the club. So can you make it quick, darling?"

Once inside the gaudy lounge, dominated by an orange carpet, Grace got straight to the point.

"It's about Zena acting out a fantasy for 'Boris'. You said she told you about it, but you described in such detail how she pretended to be innocent and let herself be seduced, it was like you were actually there."

"You're very sharp, darling. I wasn't there, but Zena did more than just tell me about it. She'd recorded a tape of her role play with Boris and gave me a copy of it."

"Why did she do that? Were you two planning to blackmail him?"

"Good heavens, no! If she'd something like that in mind, she would've videoed it, wouldn't she? No, she sometimes recorded her sessions with clients for a bit of fun. This one was a real scream – she gave me a copy so that I could have a good laugh. Mind you, I also found it a turn-on."

"Have you still got the tape?"

"Yes, I'll get it for you."

*****

Grace spent most of the afternoon shopping and visiting a travel agent to find out about flight details to Senegal so that she would be prepared if her mother's condition became worse.

Once back in her flat, she found that her hunger pangs outweighed her desire to hear the tape. That prompted her to heat up a ready-made chilli and rice in the microwave and enjoy her first meal of the day with some wine.

Grace then showered and changed into silk pyjamas before pouring another glass of wine, which she took into her bedroom together with the tape and a machine to play it on. She sipped some of the wine, flopped on the bed – and promptly fell asleep.

CHAPTER FORTY-FIVE

Saturday, 12 October 2013

Livermore kept his promise to accompany Agnes to their nephew's wedding in Twickenham on Saturday and did not get to read the murder story until very late in the day.

That was because his sturdy, straight-talking, no-nonsense wife had confiscated the morning paper from him!

"You're nae having that!" she yelled as he started to pull it out of the letter box after oversleeping and coming down late. She forced her way past him and snatched the paper.

"Just let me have it a minute," he pleaded, tugging at it.

"No – we'll be late." She refused to let go, and the front page tore in half.

"Damn!" he snapped.

"Don't raise your voice to me, Harvey. And don't took at me like that."

He hated it when she accused him of glaring at her because he hadn't a clue if he was guilty of doing so or whether she was exaggerating.

She was now in full flow. "If you wanted to read newspapers, you should've come down earlier. They're only full of gossip anyway."

"Agnes, I'm in the middle of a vital investigation, trying to find a serial killer."

"And don't I know it? You never have any time for me anymore, Harvey. This is your day off – leave things to your staff. Either you get ready now and come to the wedding with me so that we avoid the indignity of arriving late or I go by myself. And if I do, you'll need to find time for a court date when I divorce you."

"There's no need to be like that, Agnes," he urged, putting his arm around her and attempting to kiss her on the cheek.

"Don't come near me with all that bristle," she replied, pushing him away. "Your rough face will make my chin sore. You may fool your workmates that you've got designer stubble, but the truth is you're just too lazy to shave regularly. Now go upstairs and have one."

"All right," he said, holding up his hands in surrender. "But let's have no more silly talk about a divorce."

"It's not silly, Harvey. You're so engrossed in your work I hardly see anything of you, and when you're with me, you don't listen to a word I say. I've given up expecting you to talk to me. So for you to risk making us late by reading this paper is the last straw."

"OK, you've made your point. Today I'll be the perfect attentive husband."

"We'll see. Just remember you're on probation."

"Yes, dear." He shuddered at the thought of what his colleagues would say if they could see their commanding officer reduced to a gibbering wreck by his wife.

Livermore lived up to his end of the bargain until mid-afternoon when he clearly broke one of the terms of the 'probation' Agnes had imposed on him.

He had two mobiles in his pocket – the one he always used and the 'spare' he had bought solely for Katrina to contact him on. He hadn't switched them to 'silent', and during the wedding reception, one went off as the best man was finishing his speech!

'Good grief! Is Katrina trying to reach me? Is she in danger?'

He hurriedly pulled both phones out of his coat pocket and was relieved to find the one that was ringing was not the special 'hot line' for Katrina. He fumbled to switch the ringtone off, but in his haste he pressed the wrong button, and accidentally deleted the call.

Suddenly the two mobiles were seized from his grasp. "I'll take those," said Agnes.

"Not that one," he protested, grabbing back the 'hot line'. "I'll switch it to 'vibrate' instead of 'ring'. He did so while she glared at him and dropped the other phone into her handbag.

Livermore began to speak, but his wife held up her hand to silence him. "You and your phones are stressing me out, Harvey. Just for once, let me relax and enjoy myself in your company. Please – no more calls while we're here."

He was about to argue when Agnes's sister Mary butted in. "Come on, Harvey, unwind and pay your wife some attention."

The policeman, realising that O'Sullivan was on duty and could contact Nottage if there was a problem, reluctantly relented, safe in the knowledge that he still had the other phone in his possession – and it would vibrate if Katrina needed him.

When the speeches were over, Agnes rounded on Harvey once more. "Why have you got two mobiles? Is one to take calls from some fancy woman you're seeing?"

"Don't be bloody stupid, woman," he snapped. "What time have I got for an affair?"

His afternoon got worse when Aunt Hilda bumped into him, knocking her glass of red wine over his jacket, which he had to take off while a waiter sponged it. When he put it back on, it was still wet, and the stain passed on to his shirt.

Livermore was on the receiving end of more rough justice on the way home that evening. His wife devoted half the car journey to dishing out what he called HVS – horrendous verbal stick!

Most of her tirade was delivered in a thick Scottish accent, emphasising how upset she was with him.

"Nobody else left their phones on, Harvey."

"Perhaps that's because nobody else is a senior police officer in the middle of investigating a murder," he pointed out, taking two aspirins. "I do love you, Agnes, but you drive me bloody mad. I'd rather take on a villain and risk GBH than receive HVS from you."

When they arrived home, Agnes finally surrendered his main mobile phone, and he got to see the paper containing Ross Yardley's story.

Holding the torn page together, he exploded as he read the headline, 'SERIAL KILLER COULD STRIKE AGAIN', followed by the subsidiary heading, 'Victims cut with commando knife'.

"Damn and blast it!" he raged, screwing up the paper and hurling it towards the waste-paper bin. It missed and ended up on the floor. "Who the devil gave them the very information I wanted withheld?"

His tantrum was interrupted by the startled voice of his wife. "Harvey, have you resorted to talking to yourself?"

"Yes, I have – and is it any wonder? One of my team has defied my orders and given this journalist Ross Yardley almost every detail about the latest murder. The bastard has even printed how the attacker cut the chins of all three victims to try to force them to submit to his sexual demands before killing them."

"Calm down, Harvey – you'll give yourself a heart attack. Does it matter that much?"

Livermore almost erupted again. "Of course, it matters. This story will encourage more cranks to claim to be the killer. And, worse still, it will scare women into believing that they could be the next victim. Someone is going to pay for this."

It was only then that he checked his two mobiles. He was unable to trace the call he had deleted from his main line and would check with the office in the morning, but when he looked at the 'hot line', he was horrified to find there was a missed call. He had obviously not felt the bloody thing vibrating in his jacket pocket – or the call had come during the few minutes his jacket was being sponged down.

CHAPTER FORTY-SIX

Saturday, 12 October 2013

Suzie phoned her sister on Saturday evening for a chat and mentioned that she'd seen Katrina's 'new boyfriend' earlier that day.

"Are you referring to Justin?" asked Katrina.

"I certainly am. He didn't have much to say to me. In fact, he seemed completely different to earlier in the week when he was gushing compliments to both of us."

"Where did you meet him?"

"At the optician's when I went to get some new lenses this morning."

"So Justin needed glasses too?"

"No, silly. He WAS the optician."

"WHAT? He never said anything about being an optician. He told me he was a financial adviser."

"Perhaps he lied to you, Katrina."

"Why would he do that? It seems rather bizarre."

"Well," confessed Suzie, "I found it odd too, because he didn't recognise me. I had to remind him that you'd introduced us. Even then he wasn't at all chatty or charming like he'd been when he offered us a lift."

"That's most peculiar," agreed her sister. "Are you positive it was Justin?"

"I'm quite sure, unless he has a twin brother. He hasn't, has he?"

"Not that I'm aware of."

"Well, if he has, I know how to tell them apart," Suzie informed her. "The optician told me to focus on one of his ears when he was examining my eyes, and I noticed he'd a scar on it. It was shaped almost like a horseshoe. Presumably that's unique to him."

CHAPTER FORTY-SEVEN

Saturday, 12 October 2013

Katrina sat puzzled in her flat, mulling over the telephone conversation she'd just had with her sister.

She couldn't believe that Justin was an optician because he'd only talked to her about his work as a financial adviser. And it seemed weird that he didn't recognise Suzie just a short time after Katrina had introduced him to her. He'd even given them a lift in his car!

'Could the optician be a lookalike or a twin brother? If so, maybe it was this other man who'd committed the murders.'

Katrina had not noticed whether Justin had a scar on one of his ears. She was so determined to find out that she promptly jumped in her car and drove around to visit him.

As she parked outside his flat, it suddenly dawned on her that if she was wrong – and Justin was the killer – she was putting herself in danger. She took out the mobile Livermore had given her and dialled his number. But his phone was switched off. *'To hell with it – I'll take the risk!'*

"Hello, this is a pleasant surprise," said Justin when he answered the door of his ground-floor apartment to her. "I was going to have an early night," he added by way of explaining why he was wearing pyjamas underneath a distinctive black dressing gown with a red dragon emblazoned on it. "Do come in."

Katrina sat in one of two leather armchairs while Justin fetched them both a drink. Looking around the well-furnished lounge, she noticed the furthest wall was covered with framed posters from concerts and musicals he'd presumably attended over the years.

At first their conversation was disjointed, but after each had downed a vodka and coke, they began to unwind.

It was Justin who brought up the very subject that was concerning her.

"I'm surprised you're still seeing me. You must've read that a third woman from our dating agency has been murdered."

"Yes, I have. Did you know her?"

"Only slightly – I met her at the social function I told you about. But the police have been focusing on male members from the agency, and I'm their main suspect. They took me into custody and gave me a real grilling. They also searched my property and took away my clothing and every pair of bloody shoes I own. I thought I was going to be charged, but instead they let me go. They didn't explain why."

"You've got me to thank for that. I told Chief Inspector Livermore that you'd given me and my sister Suzie a lift to the cinema on Monday so you couldn't have been in Brighton killing someone."

"Thanks for getting me off the hook. My mind was in such a whirl when the police were firing questions at me that I didn't recall it was on Monday I bumped into you in Eastbourne. I couldn't remember where I was. How did the police come to ask you?"

Katrina had to think quickly. She could hardly reveal to Justin that she'd offered her services to Livermore to try to trap him. "I phoned them. I heard on TV that you'd been arrested, so I rang the police to tell them you'd been with me."

"That was very good of you. No wonder they were livid at having to let me go. They thought I'd committed the other two murders as well, you know."

"But you didn't, did you?"

"No, I didn't. I'm no killer, and I don't think you'd be sitting here if you believed I was."

There followed an uneasy silence. Justin ended it by exclaiming, "The police must be well pissed off. My solicitor Muriel Bellington has given them a really hard time. She says they call her the Rottweiler because she never lets up. And she delights in exploiting their mistakes."

"What mistakes would they be?"

"Oh, there were flaws in their DNA evidence, and the Rottweiler was quick to pounce on it. She's been a real pain to them. Muriel told me this hilarious story about how she got one of her clients off a drink-driving charge. A copper alleged that her client had admitted to being 'half pissed'. What she claimed he'd actually said was that he was a harpist!"

Katrina burst out laughing, but she was still on edge. Unfortunately, the dim lighting prevented her taking a good look at Justin's ears. She'd have to find an excuse to get close to him, so she went over to look at his posters and, upon returning, sat on the arm of his chair. Katrina bent down to kiss him on the cheek while running her fingers over his left ear, and found no trace of a scar.

Now for the right ear! But before she could reach it, Justin pulled her on to his lap and kissed her on the lips.

As the kiss deepened, Katrina felt his thumb tracing the contours of her left breast over her black silk blouse. She allowed him to undo two of the buttons while she tried to move her hand towards his right ear, but he was leaning against her arm, preventing her from doing so.

Justin had found his way into her blouse, and a third button popped open as his fingers moved inside her low-cut black lace bra to stroke her ample left bosom. Before she could stop him, he began massaging her pert, pink nibble.

Katrina realised this was the best chance she would get to check for a horseshoe-shaped marking, so she let him continue playing with her breast while she nibbled at his ear. No scar!

Now she could push him off. But she was feeling an unexpected arousal as he bent his head forward and gently circled his tongue over her enlarged bud. Instead of rejecting him, she ran her fingers through his hair as he started to suck her aching nipple.

Justin raised his head, and for a moment their eyes met, both full of desire, and within seconds he was kissing her firmly on the lips again. He then placed his hand between Katrina's knees and edged it slowly up her left leg. "No," she murmured, trying to come to her senses.

He showed little sign of obeying her half-hearted plea. She tried to close her legs, but the persistent hand continued on its upward journey, reaching the soft flesh of her thighs.

"No," she repeated again, "you're going too far."

"Are you sure?"

Katrina made no further protest. She knew it was too late because his eager fingers had discovered she was wearing only a skimpy G-string. Her wetness had made the material moist, betraying how much she was turned on.

They slid on to the carpeted floor, locked together, with Katrina's skirt now around her waist and Justin's dressing gown falling open.

Her legs had parted, and within seconds he was pushing aside the G-string and pleasuring her with his fingers.

Katrina was feeling a mixture of euphoria, guilt, and confusion.

'How can I be allowing this man, who I'd previously found unattractive, to do this to me?'

Justin eventually changed his position so that she could reach the slit in his pyjamas. She slid her hand inside, releasing his now-massive tool, and ran her fingertips along it. Her feather-light touch caused him to moan.

Katrina mischievously caressed his balls gently with her other hand but increased the pressure on his cock.

"Oh, my poor dick."

"Would you like me to stop?" she teased.

"Well, if you continue to do that, it will explode."

"Let's not waste it," Katrina murmured.

"Then you'd better be quick. Put it inside you before it comes."

The cock was so huge it seemed to stretch her to breaking point.

Katrina gasped in pain – but mainly in ecstasy – as they both climaxed.

CHAPTER FORTY-EIGHT

Saturday, 12 October 2013

As Katrina lay next to Justin, a phone started ringing. The sound was coming from her bag – it was the mobile Livermore had given her. She answered it and found herself speaking to a very concerned chief inspector.

"No, I'm OK," she assured him. "I can't talk now, but I'm fine. I'll be in touch."

As she rang off, she could see Justin looking at her quizzically.

"It was just my sister," she lied.

'Thank goodness Livermore did not call earlier or he'd have caught us at it. If he knew what had occurred, he'd be livid. I took a big risk coming to Justin's flat without the police on hand. But far from attacking me, he gave me the best sex I've had for ages. Correction: the ONLY sex I've had for ages!'

"That was fantastic," Justin told her.

"You liked it then?" she said, mockingly.

"You were wonderful," he replied, gently kissing her forehead as they sat together on the floor. "Quite wonderful. And to find you weren't wearing any panties made it an even bigger turn-on."

"I seldom do, unless I'm in a split skirt, like I was when we went to the theatre. I usually wear a G-string or bikini briefs – occasionally nothing at all."

Justin shook his head. "It was a surprise. I thought you were demure and very ladylike."

"I am. I just don't like wearing panties. It dates back to when I wet my knickers at primary school and was forced to keep them on for the rest of the day. I've just got a 'thing' about it. The 'up' side is that I don't have to worry about a panty line showing."

They laughed.

"Just like you have an aversion to panties, I hate scarves and polo neck jumpers," Justin confided. "I can't bear anything hugging my neck."

"Anything else I should know about you? Any hidden secrets?"

"Not really. But I'm superstitious. When I play football or cricket, I always take the field last. And I put on my right sock first. But I read that Cristiano Ronaldo also does that when he's preparing for a match, so I'm in good company."

"And does it work?"

"Are you kidding? It's made him probably the best footballer in the world!"

"No, I meant does it work for you?"

"Unfortunately not – I'm crap at both football and cricket."

Katrina decided this was the ideal time to ask what had been on her mind from the moment she'd left home. "Justin, do you have a twin brother?"

"What makes you say that?"

"I'll tell you once you answer my question," she said, flashing him another of her dazzling smiles.

"Yes, I do. His name is Montgomery, but he's known as Monty. So what makes you ask?"

"And are you identical twins?"

"Yes, we are."

"He's an optician, isn't he?"

"That's right. What's this? Twenty questions about my brother? Have you met him?"

"No, I haven't, but my sister Suzie has. She went to get new lenses, and he was the optician. She thought it was you."

"That's not surprising – we still look exactly the same. So that explains all your questions."

"Not entirely. Doesn't it occur to you that if you didn't do the murders, it could've been someone who looks exactly like you?"

"You're suggesting that Monty might be the murderer?" he said, laughing in derision.

"What's so funny?"

"It's utterly preposterous. For a start, the police believe the killer is a member of the dating agency, and Monty doesn't belong to it. Furthermore, Monty's not a lady's man. He prefers men. I shouldn't think he's been sexually aroused by a woman since our schooldays when our gym teacher's knicker elastic broke."

The joke brought a big smile from Katrina. But she soon became serious again and insisted, "Just because Monty's a homosexual doesn't rule him out."

CHAPTER FORTY-NINE

Sunday, 13 October 2013

Livermore's miserable weekend got even worse when he read the Sunday papers in bed.

Yardley had flogged a follow-up story to the tabloids, claiming that two killers could be on the loose.

"Where the hell did he get that from?" the policeman yelled to nobody in particular, but causing his wife to wake from her slumbers.

The story revealed that the first two murder victims had received anal injuries but that Zena Cattermole had not. This prompted Yardley to draw the conclusion there might be two killers.

He went on to speculate that the third murder could have been a 'copycat' on the basis that all three women had first been cut under the chin to force them to have sex.

"You've got that bloody well wrong, buddy!" rasped Livermore as he continued to talk to himself. "Zena didn't have sex with her attacker."

Yardley's story even made reference to the fact that he understood dark brown hairs had been found on the victim that may belong to the killer. He claimed that this could not be confirmed because 'Detective Chief Inspector Harvey Livermore was not available for comment'.

Livermore was furious. "When I find out who is responsible for these leaks, they'll wish they'd never been born," he snapped.

"Do be quiet, Harvey," mumbled Agnes, whose scowling face suggested to him that her 'beauty sleep' had not worked.

*****

A disgruntled Livermore went into his study to deal with the calls on his answerphone. Stella Rudd from the police press office had phoned him twice the previous day, leaving messages for him to get back to her, but her mobile had been turned off when he had tried to do so late last night. He rang her number again.

"Stella," he said when she answered on the fifth ring, "you wanted me." Before she could reply, he added, "Have you seen this bloody story in this morning's papers?"

"I have indeed, Chief Inspector." Her soothing tone calmed him down, and he smiled as he reflected that poor Stella had been at the back of the queue when good looks were given out, but she had a voice as smooth as velvet.

"Do you know where they got their facts from?" he asked.

"No, I don't. I was bombarded with calls from the press yesterday, asking for confirmation about the story they were planning to run. I phoned you three times, but you weren't at home, and my call to your mobile was not accepted. I couldn't deny the claims that we were looking for a 'copycat' because you hadn't briefed me. Presumably you were tied up most of yesterday. Anything I should know about?"

"No," he said curtly, silently cursing his wife for giving him so much grief the previous day and causing him to accidentally delete Stella's call to his mobile.

"Well, is the story true?"

"Parts of it are, but the stuff about a copycat is pure speculation. Someone from my team or the forensics department must've leaked details about our findings. This has done one hell of a lot of damage. Yardley has twisted the facts to suit himself. He claimed in his story yesterday that all three murders had been committed by a serial killer, but today he's saying that we have a copycat."

"Yes, but unfortunately, Yardley's contradictory reports also contain several facts to make them sound convincing," Stella pointed out. "To add to the confusion, there was a story given out on one of the regional radio stations yesterday about a woman being stabbed in Horsham. The bright spark of a radio reporter suggested that the serial killer might have struck again. I checked with the police in Horsham, and it was a 'domestic'. The woman was stabbed by her husband and is recovering in hospital. So I presume you'd be happy for me to put out a press release saying this has no connection to the murders."

"Yes, of course. I just wish I'd been available yesterday. These stories about killers on the loose must be putting the fear of God into every woman in Sussex."

"I can issue a second press release this morning, quoting you, to further dispel these fears," Stella responded. "I'll put something together and email it to you for your approval."

"That would be most helpful. You can quote me as saying that if it should emerge Zena Cattermole was murdered by a different man from the previous two victims, we have no reason to believe he will kill again. But whether we're looking for one man or two, we're making good progress with our investigation and hope to bring charges soon."

"Will do," the press officer confirmed. "I'll send you a draft and see that something goes out within the next hour."

"Thank you, Stella. This damn reporter Yardley is a right pain. He doesn't care about writing conflicting stories as long as they make him money."

"That's about the size of it, Chief Inspector. Yardley obviously felt he needed to come up with a completely different angle for the Sundays to ensure his story got used."

Livermore's tone lightened. "Presumably you're at home trying to enjoy a day off – sorry to spoil it."

"No problem, sir."

"It's much appreciated, dear girl. You're a saint. Goodbye for now."

As Livermore put down the phone, he became aware that his wife had entered the room. He did not have to be a detective to know from her facial expression that she was offended.

"Who was that lassie you were chatting to so affectionately, Harvey, and calling a saint? Was I right about you carrying on with someone behind my back?"

"If you saw Stella Rudd, you wouldn't make such a suggestion. She resembles a saint all right – but unfortunately a St Bernard!"

"Who is she?"

"Stella's our press officer. She'd been trying to contact me urgently yesterday about the murder case but couldn't speak to me because we were at the wedding and you confiscated my bloody phone."

"Please don't swear, Harvey. So it was this press officer who phoned your mobile during the best man's speech. That was so inconsiderate of her."

"How was she to know she was interrupting the speeches?" Livermore reasoned, exasperated.

His wife's blank expression gave him no indication as to whether she had detected from his tone of voice how annoyed he was becoming.

"Well," she said, "I'm sure that young lassie must've understood why you couldn't talk to her yesterday. You did tell her you were at a wedding, didn't you?"

Livermore could bottle his agitation no longer. "No, Agnes, I didn't tell her. If I had, I still don't think she would have understood why I didn't phone her back sometime during the day – and I'm damn sure Detective Superintendent Frampton wouldn't."

After his wife had stormed out of the room, the careworn copper glanced in the mirror and shook his head. "No wonder I have bags under my eyes and am starting to go grey," he said. "And now I'm talking to myself again. Perhaps I'm heading for a breakdown."

CHAPTER FIFTY

Sunday, 13 October 2013

The sound of the Sunday newspaper dropping through the letter box caused Grace to wake up with a start.

She promptly chastised herself for not listening to the tape that Pixie had given her. Never mind, she could do so this morning – but first she fetched the paper.

"Oh no!" she exclaimed when she saw Yardley's story, revealing even more facts gleaned from her notebook. She tried to lighten her mood by flicking through the magazine supplement that had come with the paper. An interview with best-selling crime novelist Peter James caught her eye. He was pointing out that serial killers are usually presentable, cunning chameleons who blend into the environment so well that they are undetected for years.

'*Whether it's two killers or one we're looking for, it's going to be bloody difficult to find them,*' she thought.

She needed something to raise her spirits. So she retrieved the unfinished bottle of wine, poured herself a full glass, and took a couple of sips. Then she switched on the tape recording and lay back on her bed to listen to it.

The tape started with a man explaining in a rich, deep voice – just like the pompous oaf of a solicitor Boris Kimble's – that he wanted Anna Marie to act the part of his shy, naive girlfriend called Suzie, and slowly let him seduce her.

When the role play began, the man again took the initiative, telling 'Suzie' that it was time for her to change from being 'a frightened virgin' to a 'provocative temptress'.

Boris: "First, I want you to cross your legs seductively so that your skirt rises . . . a little more, please."

A brief silence followed.

Boris: "That's great, Suzie. Seeing a flash of those red suspenders is having a big effect on me already. Eventually, you'll be confident enough to do this in front of other men too."

It made Grace angry. "You stupid male-chauvinistic bastard!" she hissed before taking a mouthful of wine. "You're a bigger wanker than Ross fucking Yardley."

She had to stop and rewind the tape to hear Anna Marie protesting, "I couldn't possibly."

Grace's mind briefly drifted to her sexual experience with Ross, and she missed a snatch of the dialogue but heard Boris saying something about 'Suzie' having men begging for more, wondering whether she was revealing her suspenders by accident or on purpose.

"Fucking men!" Grace muttered under her breath. "You sods just regard us as sex objects."

Boris was now saying, "It's because you're shy and innocent. Your reluctance and uncertainty make you the perfect tease. If some women flashed the flesh, it would have little effect on a man because they'd look cheap and tacky, but others, like you, are real class."

Grace took another large gulp of wine before putting down the glass. She was feeling light-headed and subconsciously began to finger the top button of her cream silk pyjamas.

Anna Marie: "I find that hard to believe, Boris."

Boris: "You want proof? Come over here."

There was a sound of 'Suzie' getting up and walking towards him.

Boris: "Give me your hand . . . Can you feel how hard I am? You've done that to me simply by flashing your lovely legs. Let me see them again. Lift up your skirt . . . higher, my darling – now let me see your panties."

As Grace listened more intently to the tape, she found herself becoming turned on, and slowly undid the button she'd been fiddling with.

Boris: "What will I see if you move your panties to one side? Will there be hairs or a shaven pussy?"

Anna Marie: "I can't talk like that."

Boris: "Of course, you can. Tell me."

Anna Marie: "There's some hairs."

Boris: "Show me! Move your panties."

In the silence that followed, Grace gave in to temptation and unfastened another button, partly exposing one of her large soft breasts.

Boris: "Don't be a prick tease, darling."

Grace's left hand moved inside the loose material of her pyjama top to caress her heaving breasts in turn. She sighed as her large dark nipples hardened.

Boris: "You naughty girl, Suzie. You've cut your pubic hairs into the cutest little heart. You hussy. And you're wet, aren't you?"

"Yes, you fucking bastard, I am," Grace sighed, softly fingering herself through her pyjamas.

Anna Marie: "Sorry. I'm so ashamed."

Boris: "Don't be ashamed – it's great. Now ask me if I'd like you to take your panties down."

Anna Marie: "Must I?"

Boris: "Just do it, darling."

Anna Marie: "Boris, would you like me to take my panties down?"

Boris: "Yes, that would be nice. Please remove your panties."

A short silence was followed by heavy breathing. Grace realised it was her own as she began to massage one of her stiff, erect nipples until it hurt. Her other hand moved inside her pyjama bottoms and stroked the top of one of her smooth glistening thighs before reaching her groin.

Boris: "You look wonderful, Suzie."

Anna Marie: "Thank you."

It was the softly spoken 'thank you' that did it. Grace became even more aroused. Her fingers eagerly pushed down her pyjama bottoms, and she stroked her public hairs.

Boris: "Now ask if I'd like to touch you between your legs and pleasure you."

Anna Marie: "I can't, Boris. Please don't make me do that."

Boris: "Nonsense! I want you to say: 'Boris, would you like to play with my pussy?'"

Anna Marie (stammering): "Boris, would you . . . would you like to play with my pus . . . pussy?"

Boris: "Yes, I would."

Grace's long, sleek fingers made their way to her own pussy, and she gasped as she touched her wetness.

Boris: "Look what you've done to me . . . Pull down the zip and feel inside."

There was a sound of rustling before Boris spoke again. "My cock is rigid. Take it out . . . Stroke it! . . . Now you've got a choice – you can either put the cock in your fanny or, better still, you can suck it off."

Anna Marie: "I c . . . c . . . can't. Please don't ask me to do that."

During the silence on the tape Grace leaned across to her bedside cabinet and grasped the long pink wand that had served her so well in the past. She put the vibrator on 'slow' and placed it deep into her sensitive opening, sliding it smoothly in and out until her muscles clenched around the shaft.

Boris: "Keep licking – that's fantastic . . . Now take it in your mouth – all of it . . . Pretend it's a lollipop and suck it, darling."

As the young policewoman's sexual desire became more intense, she turned the sex toy to 'fast' and used it to rub her G-spot. Grace began to moan softly – then louder and louder.

The rubbing became more frantic. Her body went rigid, and she arched backwards, shrieking in ecstasy.

Throwing the vibrator aside, she stroked her pussy with her fingers, making the most of the last few climactic thrusts. Then she lay spent, hands resting on her belly, enjoying the lingering sensation.

"Who needs bloody men?" she said, reaching for the bottle of wine.

CHAPTER FIFTY-ONE

Monday, 14 October 2013

Although Livermore had calmed down somewhat by Monday morning, he was still angry – and determined to reprimand whoever had stitched him up.

A rain cloud followed him all the way to work, and by the time he got there, the heavens had erupted, leaving him drenched, with his hair dripping and plastered to his head. His mood now matched the weather.

He checked his emails, and a missive from Frampton added to his annoyance. It demanded, "What's going on? Are we looking for one killer or two?"

The unfortunate Dimbleby made the mistake of being the first member of the team to arrive and was given a grilling by his disgruntled senior officer.

Dimbleby was obliged to issue a stream of denials. No, he had not spoken to the press. No, he'd not revealed to anyone the type of weapon used by the killer. No, he'd not talked, even to his wife, about how the killer had first cut his victims under the chin to intimidate them.

Livermore did not let up. "But have you revealed to anyone outside the office that the first two victims suffered anal penetration?"

"No, Gov."

"Or have you, perhaps, mentioned the theory that there could be two killers?"

"I can assure you, Governor, that I haven't said anything to anybody."

It was not until fifteen minutes later that Nottage brought Conteh into the chief inspector's office to 'confess'.

"I can't believe it!" stormed Livermore after listening stony-faced to what she'd done. "You not only had a relationship with this newspaper reporter Ross Yardley, but you invited him into your flat and let him read your notes on the case. This is utterly irresponsible behaviour."

She bowed her head.

"Have you anything to say, Conteh?"

There was no response.

Livermore made a fist and used his other hand to crack his knuckles. "In your own time, Conteh."

She looked up, but before she could answer, Nottage came to her defence. "With respect, Gov, Conteh was not aware that Yardley had access to her notebook. She told me that only after the story appeared on Saturday did she realise that Yardley had looked inside her handbag and found her notes in it."

"How did he happen to come across the handbag?" Livermore asked harshly.

Conteh found her voice. "Yardley saw it on the floor while he was alone in my lounge, and I was cooking dinner for us. I didn't willingly give him any information about the case."

"Please, spare me the excuses, Conteh. You couldn't have made it much easier for Yardley if you'd HANDED your notes to him. He's even printed that brown hairs were found on the victim – something else we didn't want known. Presumably you'd also put in your notebook that the third victim did not suffer an anal injury as the first two had done, and that we could be looking for two killers?"

"I scribbled down a reference to the injuries . . . but I didn't make a definite conclusion. I just put a footnote posing the question 'one killer or two'?"

Livermore shook his head. "Obviously that was sufficient for Yardley to write one story about a serial killer and another story about a copycat. Women must be worried sick that they could be the next victim. It's also had an adverse effect on our investigation. I can't overlook this, Conteh."

There was a long silence as he considered his options. "Just how serious is this relationship you have with Yardley?"

"It's now non-existent," she spluttered, lifting her head. "When I saw the story on Saturday, I told him what an arsehole he was – I won't be seeing him again."

"Well, at least that's something, but I'm seriously considering taking you off the case. You should never have associated so closely with a reporter."

"I didn't intend to," Conteh said lamely. "I bumped into him when DI Nottage and I went to see the student who owned the car in which Protheroe was shot. Ross called out to me and reminded me that we used to go to the same school – in fact, we were classmates – so I agreed to see him to discuss old times. I'm very sorry. As DI Nottage has already made clear to me, it was a bad error of judgement."

"And you appear to have made another one in going to see this nightclub dancer Pixie on your own without informing a senior officer. You should've notified DI Nottage instead of taking things upon yourself. But you did show excellent detection qualities in discovering the existence of a tape recording and obtaining it."

Livermore's mood lightened somewhat, helped by the fact his hair and clothing had now dried out. The tone of his voice softened as he said, "In the circumstances, and considering that we're low on manpower, especially as DC Yedding is on sick leave, I'll let you stay on this investigation. But if you step out of line again, then I'll throw the book at you. And you can be sure it will be a very heavy book!"

Conteh was then asked to play the tape recording of 'Boris' and 'Suzie' to her two senior officers, after which the three of them discussed how deep the solicitor might be involved.

"The existence of a tape could support the theory that Zena Cattermole was blackmailing Kimble," said Livermore.

Conteh spoke up. "It's possible, but, as Pixie pointed out, if Zena's motive was blackmail, she would surely have videoed the session. She just recorded it for a laugh."

"Laughter was not the emotion it brought out in me," admitted Nottage. "More like raw lust. Surely, it would've the same effect on most people, male or female." He looked across at Conteh, but the policewoman didn't meet his gaze.

Livermore spared her from possible embarrassment by summing up the situation. "Despite what Pixie claims, Zena could've been blackmailing Kimble. That would've given him sufficient reason to murder Zena in a copycat killing, but it's hard to imagine him actually doing so."

"After listening to the tape, I believe he's capable of it, Gov," Nottage argued. "Not only did Kimble have the motive to commit murder, he also had the imagination to make it look like the work of a serial killer. Actually, it wouldn't have taken too much imagination. As a solicitor, he could've seen reports giving full details on how the first two murders were carried out. It would've been like stumbling upon a blueprint!"

"Yes," added Conteh, "and we must presume he had the opportunity as well because he refused to tell us where he was last Monday night."

Livermore nodded. "OK, it could fit. But you need to provide some facts to support your theory. Invite Kimble to come in to help provide a clearer picture about Zena Cattermole and the men she was seeing. He's a clever bastard who knows how to use the letter of the law to his advantage, so use a subtle approach."

CHAPTER FIFTY-TWO

Monday, 14 October 2013

When Nottage phoned Kimble to ask him to come into the police station, the solicitor expressed his annoyance.

"I've already told you all I can," he snapped.

"We simply need to ask you further questions to assist us with our murder enquiry, Mr Kimble."

"This is nothing short of police harassment. I intend to complain to your superiors."

So it was that Livermore had the 'pleasure' of welcoming an agitated legal practitioner later that day.

"I'm very upset," Kimble informed him. "I've told your officers I didn't know the murdered woman, either as Zena Cattermole or Anna Marie, yet they still want to ask me questions about her. I wish to make a complaint."

"You are quite at liberty to do so, Mr Kimble. But I'm not happy with some aspects of your statement to my officers. We can deal with this as a voluntary attendance, but I need to ask you further questions under caution, which I propose to do now."

This resulted in Kimble accompanying Livermore and DC Conteh to the Voluntary Attendance Suite, a small room wired for sound and video, with a camera set in two corners. Conteh operated a touch screen computer while Livermore asked the questions.

First, he issued a caution by saying, "Boris Kimble, you are not under arrest. You do not have to say anything, but it may harm your defence if you fail to mention when questioned something which you later rely on in court. Anything you do say may be given in evidence. I must also advise you that you are entitled to consult a solicitor and are free to leave at any time.

"Now, Mr Kimble, I want to ask you about Zena Cattermole. Did you meet her at the Krazy Knights nightclub where she was known as Anna Marie?"

"Not that I'm aware of."

"We believe you did, and that you subsequently hired Anna Marie to act out a sexual fantasy for you."

"That's an outrageous suggestion. I'll be complaining . . ."

The chief inspector held up his hand, interrupting him. "We have a tape recording of the whole role play between the two of you."

Kimble looked shocked, but he continued to protest. "A tape recording isn't proof."

"Not only does Anna Marie call the man on the tape 'Boris', but he has a deep, rich voice just like yours."

"It could be almost anyone," Kimble insisted, rising to his feet. "I'm not prepared to sit here listening to this nonsense, Chief Inspector. I've got better things to do with my time." He walked towards the door.

Livermore announced that the interview was suspended and signalled to Conteh to turn off the equipment.

"As you're unable to confirm it was you on the tape, we'll have to make an appeal to the public to help us identify this man. That will entail us making part of the recording available to the media, including radio and TV stations."

"That would be most unethical."

"Not at all. This is a murder enquiry, and we're entitled to have part of the tape played on TV and radio to see if any members of the public recognise the voice of someone named 'Boris' speaking to a 'girlfriend' called 'Suzie'."

"That's harassment – I'll see that you're disciplined if you pull a stunt like that."

"Well, you'll have plenty of time to gloat about me being reprimanded after you've been booted out of the Law Society and dropped like a hot potato by Suzie Merton."

Kimble was rattled. He walked back to the chair he'd been sitting in previously and crumbled into it.

"Now," instructed Livermore, "let's stop playing silly games."

He announced that the interview was resuming, after Conteh again switched on the recording and video equipment.

"It is you on the tape, isn't it, Mr Kimble?"

"Yes," admitted the solicitor, holding his head in his hands. "It's me."

The policeman simply waited. Following a brief silence, Kimble looked up and continued, "I'd met Anna Marie in the Krazy Knights. She performed a lap dance for me and made it clear she was willing to provide sex if I paid for it. At first, I politely declined her offer, but I went back there a couple of nights later and took her up on it."

"Where did you go with her?"

"She wanted to take me to a hotel, but I told her I was known there. So she said we could go back to her flat. We'd both had a few drinks by the time we got there, and my suggestion that we act out a sexual fantasy appealed to her."

"How many times did you pay Anna Marie for these extras?"

"Just the once. I only did it because my girlfriend and I weren't having sex at that time."

"Your girlfriend is Suzie Merton, I believe."

"Yes. After she was assaulted in a car park last year, she was reluctant to have a sexual relationship. I was getting frustrated, and that's why I resorted to paying Anna Marie. But since then Suzie has become a lot more responsive, so there's no longer any need for me to seek sex elsewhere. It would destroy Suzie if she found out, Chief Inspector. She doesn't have to know, does she? I made a silly mistake, and I'd do anything to keep it from her."

"It all depends on whether you remain a murder suspect, Mr Kimble."

"Murder suspect! I thought this interview was simply about establishing that it was me on the tape so you could eliminate others from your enquiries. Surely you don't seriously believe I'd have killed Anna Marie? What motive could I possibly have had?"

"As you've just admitted, you'd do anything to keep your sexual escapade from your girlfriend. If Anna Marie was blackmailing you by threatening to tell Suzie, then you would've had an excellent motive for killing her."

"She wasn't blackmailing me."

"Well, she did record your sex session."

"But I didn't know she'd done that."

"The 64,000-dollar question, Mr Kimble, is, where were you on the night Zena Cattermole, alias Anna Marie, was murdered? That would be last Monday between 8.30 p.m. and 9.30 p.m."

"That's easy," answered a clearly relieved Kimble, apparently regaining his composure. "I was being initiated as a new member of the local Masonic lodge. There are plenty of people who can vouch for me, including your Detective Superintendent Frampton, who was among those members present."

'Bloody hell,' thought Livermore. 'It seems Nottage and Conteh have got it completely wrong.'

CHAPTER FIFTY-THREE

Monday, 14 October 2013

Livermore regretted he'd agreed to give a media briefing following the latest turn of events.

Boris Kimble seemed to have a perfect alibi, and just before the press conference was due to start at 4 p.m., O'Sullivan informed the chief inspector that Carl Tarbutt had now provided a satisfactory account of where he was on the night of the murder.

"Tarbutt didn't want me to question his wife because he was worried she'd find out about his affair with Zena Cattermole," the Irishman explained. "But I have spoken to Mrs Tarbutt and told her we needed confirmation of her husband's movements that night. She assured me he came home at 10 p.m. – and he wasn't covered in blood. I'm sure she was telling me the truth. It's a shame she had to be alerted to her husband's hanky-panky."

"It seems you handled it in your usual tactful way, Sergeant!"

Ignoring the rebuke, O'Sullivan continued, "Tarbutt's car was spotted on a motorway camera earlier in the evening of the murder. He was on his way back from Coventry, so it's unlikely he could've got to Brighton. I don't think he's our man."

"Damn!" exclaimed Livermore. "We've eliminated two of our main suspects. But at least that seems to put paid to the copycat theory."

Instead of being able to announce to the press that the police were making excellent progress, with one or two definite leads, Livermore was on the back foot.

The briefing room was packed with thirty-four media representatives – reporters from newspapers, television, and radio, plus photographers and camera and sound crews.

Sitting next to Livermore was Fussy Frampton, who'd expressed his willingness to offer his support but whose presence was actually putting extra pressure on him.

Livermore started by dealing with the theory that they could be looking for a copycat. "We've looked into the possibility that the third murder might've been committed by a different man, but the results of our enquiries so far suggest it was not a copycat. They point to it being one man responsible for all three murders."

A series of awkward questions followed, and Livermore was forced to parry most of them with stock, non-committal replies. But Ross Yardley and his colleagues persisted in asking for confirmation about the killer's methods.

"Is it right that he cut all three of his victims under the chin?" called out a female reporter from the back of the room.

"Yes, I can confirm that was the case," Livermore said reluctantly.

"The killer obviously did that to force them to have sex with him," Yardley suggested.

"That would appear to have been his intention, but Zena Cattermole was not sexually assaulted. We believe she ran out of her flat as soon as she was threatened with the knife."

Yardley refused to be deterred. "That was not made clear to us, Chief Inspector."

Livermore took a deep breath before answering. "We tried to keep certain facts back so that our main suspects might be caught out under questioning – and to avoid us being inundated with attention-seekers making false confessions."

A reporter from Sky Television started to speak, but Yardley talked over her. "The public are entitled to know what's going on," he bellowed. "I'd respectfully suggest this case has left the police baffled and the public confused."

"Only those who've been reading your stories, Yardley," piped up a cynical hack known as Burlington Bertie, seated in the third row. "On Saturday you claimed a serial killer might strike again. Then on Sunday you said there were two killers. If anyone is baffled, it seems to be you."

The room erupted in laughter as the assembled media representatives approved of the way an arrogant, egotistical colleague had been ridiculed.

Burlington Bertie, named after the toff in the musical song because of his theatrical airs and graces, took a bow.

The frustrated Sky News representative and two other reporters shot up their hands, but the DCI had had enough. "That's it for today, ladies and gentlemen." With that, he got up and quickly departed.

Frampton, rushing off to another appointment, also made a hasty retreat and left the building before Livermore got the chance to ask him about Kimble's appearance at the Masonic lodge.

CHAPTER FIFTY-FOUR

Monday, 14 October 2013

Livermore returned to his office feeling depressed.

The intervention of Burlington Bertie had helped him deal successfully with a difficult press conference, but things could hardly be worse. His three main suspects – Justin Remington, Boris Kimble, and Carl Tarbutt – all had seemingly rock-solid alibis. It meant the investigation was floundering badly.

His thoughts were suddenly interrupted by Nottage bursting into the cramped room after the briefest of knocks on the door. Surprisingly, his young inspector had a broad smile on his face.

"What are you looking so pleased about, Nottage?"

"I'm the bearer of glad tidings, Gov. I think we've finally got the breakthrough we needed."

"Well, stop bragging about it and tell me what it is. Hopefully it's better than your theory that Boris Kimble was committing a murder at the very time he was with our superintendent."

The barb wiped away Nottage's grin, but he still spoke with enthusiasm. "While you were briefing the press, Katrina Merton phoned to say she had more information to give us following her statement. She's discovered Justin Remington has an identical twin brother – he's an optician who her sister visited on Saturday. That means, of course, the brothers not only have exactly the same appearance but also the same DNA. So I believe it's the twin, called Montgomery, who is our killer."

Livermore was stunned. "How come there's nothing about Remington having a twin on our records? I've been through Justin's file with a fine-tooth comb, and all it mentions is a brother born a year after him – not a twin. Don't tell me that the background check on him was wrong."

"Yes, it was, but there were extenuating circumstances," Nottage explained, taking a seat, uninvited. "You see, although Justin and Monty Remington are identical twins, they were born in different years."

"And just how is that possible, Jeff?"

"Their mother Gladys gave birth to Justin on the last day of the year, December 31st, 1981, shortly before midnight. There was a complication and Monty arrived two hours later, by which time it was January 1st, 1982. That's why their birth certificates show different years."

"Most unusual."

"So unusual that our checks didn't reveal Justin had a twin. Police records simply showed there was a brother, born in a different year. In fact, the admin department contributed to the confusion by entering the month incorrectly – instead of putting the first day of the first month, they added an extra 'one' and typed in the first day of the eleventh month."

"What a bloody mess!" Livermore raged. "That's the second cock up to seriously impede this investigation."

"Presumably you're referring to the mother of one of the victims contaminating the evidence, Gov?"

"Yes, that was partly why Justin Remington wasn't prosecuted."

"Surely that was a blessing in disguise, Gov. It now seems he was innocent and that Monty did the murders."

"So don't sit there talking about it. Bring him in."

CHAPTER FIFTY-FIVE

Monday, 14 October 2013

Within hours Monty Remington, accompanied by his solicitor, was in the police interview room at Hollingbury being questioned by Nottage and O'Sullivan.

Nottage did a 'double take' upon seeing that Monty looked an exact carbon copy of his brother. Not only did he have the same build, facial features, and colouring, but even his hairstyle and his mannerisms were virtually identical. It was quite uncanny.

Their new suspect agreed to provide his fingerprints and have a buccal swab taken to collect DNA from the cells on the inside of his cheek, but, like Justin, he vehemently denied going to Zena Cattermole's flat on the night she was killed.

"I don't even know the woman – I've never met her," he insisted.

"Perhaps you knew her by a different name," Nottage suggested. "In addition to belonging to a dating agency as Zena Cattermole, she was also a dancer working under the name of

Anna Marie at the Krazy Knights nightclub. Have you been to that club?"

"Yeah, I went there once with a friend."

"And while you were at the club you met Anna Marie."

"Not that I recall."

"Perhaps she did a lap dance for you?" Nottage persisted.

"Definitely not."

"Anna Marie gave some clients sexual favours for cash. Were you one of them?"

"That suggestion is even more absurd. I'm gay, so why would I want to go with a female prostitute?"

"You could be bisexual," Nottage shot back at him. "Are you saying you've never had any relationships with women?"

Monty Remington remained silent.

It was O'Sullivan's turn to challenge him. "You were seen ringing the doorbell at Anna Marie's flat by one of her neighbours immediately before she was murdered. What were you doing there?"

"It wasn't me. The witness must've got it wrong."

"Rubbish!" snapped O'Sullivan.

"Please . . .," interjected Remington's solicitor, a smartly dressed little man whose face resembled a weasel, "don't try to intimidate my client."

Nottage touched his fellow officer's arm to restrain him, then took over the questioning. "So, Mr Remington, where were you between the hours of 8.30 p.m. and 9.30 p.m. on Monday last week?"

Monty put his hand into the inside pocket of his stylish sports jacket before obviously realising that, following his arrest, he'd been relieved of his possessions. "If you hadn't confiscated my diary, I could look it up and tell you. Now let me try to remember. Ah, yes, on Monday last week I was at a meeting of the Anderida Writers group held at Alice Croft House, Eastbourne. They usually meet on Tuesdays, but I got an email to say they had a special event on Monday. The meeting was from 7.30 p.m. to about 10.30 p.m. You can check it out."

They did, and to their dismay found that the secretary of the writing group, Dotty Hardcastle, remembered seeing Monty there. She even recalled speaking to him for a few minutes around 9 p.m.

*****

Livermore finally received a full report from the lab liaison officer, who claimed a flu outbreak in his department had caused a delay.

"About bloody time!" Livermore exclaimed, skimming through a load of technical data until he got to the main points.

The bad news was that none of Justin Remington's clothes or shoes had any blood traces on them.

The DCI cursed, but his eyes lit up when he found the result for which he was looking – the dark brown hairs discovered on Zena Cattermole's body had enough similar properties to be consistent with the sample taken from Justin's.

He called Nottage into his office. "Take a look at that, Jeff. The hairs on the victim match those of Justin Remington. That means they would also match his identical twin brother Monty."

Nottage put on his glasses and read the relevant finding. "So one of the twins must be lying. Yet they both have witnesses placing them miles from the crime scene. How do you explain it, Gov?"

"I can't." Livermore's earlier optimism disappeared. "Perhaps the Rottweiler is right. The hairs on Miss Cattermole's dress only prove that either Justin or Monty was with her sometime – not necessarily on the night of the murder. It could be possible that one of them met her previously when she was wearing the same dress, and that's how their hair got on it. Of course, it's highly unlikely – but it's possible."

Nottage scratched his head in frustration. "What about the neighbour who saw Zena Cattermole open her door to a guy who looked just like one of the twins?"

Livermore sighed. "The trouble is both Justin and Monty seem to have airtight alibis. We need to go through them again and question more people who attended the writing group. After all, witnesses have been known to make mistakes. But, meanwhile, I don't think we've got enough to make a charge stick on either of the twins."

CHAPTER FIFTY-SIX

Tuesday, 15 October 2013

Tuesday's papers brought more anguish for Livermore. He was particularly upset by one headline, declaring: 'POLICE NO NEARER TO FINDING SEX FIEND'. The story was written by Yardley who claimed that the police were literally clueless!

Once again Livermore cursed and angrily threw the offending paper in his waste-paper bin.

Before he could compose himself, he was caught off guard by a phone call from Frampton.

"What the devil is going on, Harvey?" Frampton began curtly. "The press are having a field day at our expense. According to them, we haven't a clue about who committed this latest murder."

"That's untrue, sir," Livermore replied, trying to placate his boss without telling him a downright lie. "We're making progress and have some positive leads."

"I'd like to think so, Harvey, but that sounds exactly the sort of non-committal gobbledygook we say to fob off the media. First you claimed that you had enough evidence to charge Justin Remington – then you told me he's got an alibi. Now it seems there's no prospect of us charging anyone."

"I hope to be in a position to do so soon, sir," Livermore said soothingly, choosing his words carefully. "Unfortunately, it isn't the straightforward case it had seemed to be. Not only has Justin Remington been given an alibi, but so has his twin brother Monty."

"Yes, and that's another thing. You suddenly informed me yesterday that Justin has a twin brother. Why wasn't I told earlier?"

Livermore explained, and then discussed the lab report. "Obviously, the brown hairs we found on Zena Cattermole match those of not only Justin Remington but Monty Remington as well because they've got the same DNA. Unfortunately, witnesses claim they saw each of the twins several miles away in Eastbourne on the night of the murder. We're checking their alibis more thoroughly as well as the timelines. If there are any discrepancies, then one of the brothers could prove to be our murderer."

Frampton sighed loud enough for Livermore to clearly hear his displeasure. "It all seems pretty flimsy, Harvey. The CPS were right not to take Justin Remington to court last time, so you'll need to be damn certain you get enough evidence if you want to put him or his brother in the frame now. We can't afford to finish up with more egg on our faces."

"I'll make sure we're not put in that position, sir."

Frampton pressed home the point. "Having a costly trial finish in failure would leave the CPS and the police with all sorts of embarrassing questions to answer."

Livermore had to bite his lip to prevent him uttering his contemptuous thoughts. *'Never mind trying to seek justice for the victims and their families then? And preventing more women being attacked?'* Instead, he said, "We're not confining our investigation solely to the Remington brothers, and in that respect, there's one thing you can help me with, Charles. On the night of the latest murder, I understand you attended a Masonic lodge meeting, at which a solicitor called Boris Kimble was being initiated. Is that right?"

"Yes, quite right. Why do you ask?"

"We've come across a tape recording of Mr Kimble acting out a sexual fantasy with the victim on a previous occasion. So we need to make sure he has an alibi."

"You can eliminate him from your enquiries, Harvey. He was not only at the Masonic lodge meeting, he accompanied a few of us for drinks afterwards. He actually made some good points about what's needed to be sure a prosecution is sound – it's a pity you weren't able to listen to him.

"I should inform you that I've received a personal email from Mr Kimble complaining that DI Nottage has been harassing him. I intend to look into that."

"I think you'll find that such a complaint is without foundation, sir. I spoke to Mr Kimble myself after he'd been interviewed by DI Nottage and DC Conteh, and explained to him why he was part of our enquiries."

'Bloody hell, Kimble had more reason to complain about me than he did about Nottage. Presumably he sent Frampton his irate email before my little chat with him.'

Livermore confined himself to adding, "I do not consider that DI Nottage acted inappropriately."

"I'm glad to hear it. Nottage is a fine officer, but he can be a bit like a dog with a bone – he won't let go."

'Blimey. That criticism could be made of me too – and, for that matter, most of my officers. It's because they are bloody good at their jobs.' He was about to point this out, but Fussy Frampton continued, "This is Nottage's first murder investigation since he was made up to DI, isn't it?"

"Yes, sir."

"Just make sure he doesn't let his enthusiasm run away with him, Harvey. We need to cross all those t's and dot all those i's. When we charge the bastard who has killed these women, we need it to stick. We can't afford to run the risk that some slick defence barrister gets him off by claiming that the evidence is flawed or purely circumstantial. Make sure it's watertight this time."

Upon slamming down the phone, the DCI vented his frustration on the waste-paper bin by giving it a good kick that sent the receptacle crashing against the filing cabinet, scattering sweet papers, an empty sandwich packet, and polystyrene cups on the floor.

*****

When Livermore had eventually calmed down, he called a meeting of his team and asked for updates.

Nottage provided one that he didn't want to hear. "I've spoken to a second member of the Anderida Writers, and they confirm that Monty Remington was at their meeting."

There was a series of mutterings, but when Livermore called for suggestions, he was greeted with silence.

"Come on, you guys. I want your opinions. Let's have some input from you."

It was Conteh who responded. "Perhaps we've been focusing too much on the Remington twins. I'm not suggesting they should be ruled out, but maybe we ought to concentrate on the other men Zena Cattermole was seeing."

She flicked through the pages of her notebook to look them up. "Pixie mentioned a Maurice, a Vernon, and a Rick who'd all been with Zena."

Livermore looked across the room at O'Sullivan. "Michael, you and Chris were checking on the men who Zena met. Have you any news about these three?"

O'Sullivan, as usual, had an instant answer. "We tracked down the guys called Maurice and Vernon, and they've got alibis for the time of the murder. But so far we've been unable to find any Rick. He may've used a false name because there's nobody called Rick on the nightclub's list of members."

"Well, keep looking for him. Pixie Whitehurst said that he was an oddball, so we need to find him."

"Whitechurch," corrected Chris Dimbleby.

"Sorry?" asked a puzzled Livermore.

"It's Pixie Whitechurch, Gov. Not 'Whitehurst'."

Livermore tried not to show how much he resented this *'stupid bloody interruption'*. He paused for effect and to reflect. *'Dimbleby can be ridiculously pedantic at times – even more so than Fussy Frampton!'* Fortunately, 'Dim' had wrecked his chances of advancement when he once rashly corrected the detective superintendent.

"Quite so, Chris. I hope you've shown the same attention to detail in checking out those on the Sex Offenders Register who live in this area."

"I'm still working my way through it. So far I've come across only two pervs with no alibis, but we had already eliminated them as suspects when we investigated the previous two murders."

"Well, keep at it, Chris. But the priority is to find this oddball Rick. We now have DC Steve Yedding back from sick leave, so he can help you with the Sex Offenders." Livermore gestured towards Yedding, an unfortunate-looking young man with a pasty face covered in pockmarks. "What have you been up to this morning, Steve?"

"Taking confessions, Gov," croaked Yedding, who looked anything but recovered from his illness.

"What, you've solved the case on your first day back?" jested O'Sullivan.

"Unfortunately, these confessions were almost certainly hoax calls from cranks, Gov. So far five people have claimed they did the murder. The problem is they know a lot of the details from the press, so we'll have to check out their claims by conducting in depth interviews with them."

"I wonder how the press got all that information!" said Dimbleby sarcastically, shooting a glance at a clearly embarrassed Conteh.

"If there's any more leaks, there'll be hell to pay," threatened Livermore. But, in an attempt to lighten the atmosphere, he added, tongue-in-cheek, "You never know, perhaps something useful might come out of these media revelations, which at this moment appear to be damaging our investigation.

"Meanwhile, let's go over the three murders again and see if there's anything we've overlooked. All three victims had cuts under their chins, and the first two suffered either abrasions or bruises to their wrists. Denise Hollins and Jesse Singleton also had tears and swelling around the anus, where the perv sexually assaulted them with a blunt instrument before killing them. What that instrument was we don't know. Any ideas?"

"Perhaps it was some sort of stick," said O'Sullivan. "But it would've had to be something the perv could've carried easily."

"Maybe it was the sheath in which he kept his knife," suggested Dimbleby.

"But that would be too soft," O'Sullivan answered, dismissively.

"Not if it was a metal sheath," Dimbleby shot back.

"That's very good thinking, Chris," Livermore beamed. "Now have we any thoughts about the knife?"

Dimbleby seemed to be on a roll. "One of the papers speculated that it was a commando-type knife, and they could be right. The cuts were wide and deep, so it would have to be a large blade. I reckon we're talking about at least six inches – perhaps even eight."

"Trust you to add on a couple of extra inches, Chris," joked O'Sullivan. "Is that the chat-up line you use?" They all laughed.

"I suppose we've not come up with any more DNA or forensic evidence, Gov?" asked Dimbleby. "No semen, blood, or saliva?"

"Unfortunately, not," said Livermore. "We only have the hairs on Zena Cattermole's dress. Both belong to one of the Remington twins.

"While I accept Grace's point that we may have focused too much on the twins, the evidence shows one of them visited the flats of two of the victims. But both Justin and Monty have alibis for when Zena Cattermole was killed, and they could not have been in two places at the same time."

"Perhaps they could," said Conteh, seizing on the chance to get back in her boss's good books.

Everyone in the room turned to stare at her. Their faces showed looks of either puzzlement or disbelief.

"What do you mean, Grace?" asked Livermore.

"It's just occurred to me that one of the twins could've been covering for the other. As they are identical, nobody would know which one is which. Their alibis are that they were both in Eastbourne when Zena was killed, one with the Merton sisters and the other at the Anderida Writers group meeting. But it would've been possible for the same twin to give the Merton sisters a lift to the cinema and then slip into the writing group meeting immediately afterwards. The meeting at Alice Croft House was near to the cinema, so he could've easily got there within a matter of minutes. That would leave the other twin free to commit the murder."

CHAPTER FIFTY-SEVEN

Tuesday, 15 October 2013

Livermore called Nottage into his office, and they debated Conteh's suggested scenario that one twin could have impersonated the other to give him a perfect alibi while he committed the murder of Zena Cattermole.

"It's quite feasible," said Nottage. "The members at the writers group remember seeing one of the twins at their meeting, and they assumed it was Monty because he was the only one they'd met previously. But it could've been Justin. And furthermore, the Anderida members might not have noticed if he'd slipped in after the meeting had started.

"Apparently, the writers have a break for tea and coffee halfway through. As long as the man they believed to be Monty was there before then they might've thought, incorrectly, that he'd been present from the start."

"Yes, Jeff. It's possible, but is it likely? Katrina is convinced it was Justin who gave her and her sister a lift to the cinema. So if Conteh's theory is correct, then it would've been Monty who did the murder in Brighton while Justin provided alibis for them both in Eastbourne.

"There's just one problem. To make the alibis watertight, Justin would've had to know where to find the Merton sisters before he went to the writers' meeting and impersonated Monty. Katrina says she didn't tell him they were going to the cinema, so how could he possibly have known exactly where they'd be?"

"Good point, Gov. But perhaps it wasn't planned beforehand. Maybe Justin did bump into the Merton sisters by pure chance, and he then went to the Anderida Writers meeting as himself merely to listen to their guest speaker. If that was the case, it would be quite reasonable for people there just to assume he was Monty because Monty was already a member."

"Hmm," pondered Livermore. "So you're suggesting Justin hadn't planned to provide an alibi at all. But when he found out that Monty had committed the murder, he covered up for him. Maybe Monty phoned him and asked him to do so. It's a theory well worth considering."

They were interrupted by the phone ringing. Livermore answered it, and after listening intently, the DCI smiled broadly. He uttered, "Very many thanks indeed" before ringing off.

"That's very interesting," he informed Nottage. "The video ID parade has been held, and our witness Miss Smithson has picked out the picture of Justin Remington as the man who called on Zena Cattermole at 8.20. It could, of course, have been his identical twin she saw.

"We'll need to speak again to some of those who were present at the writers' meeting. It's possible that they too were actually seeing a double."

CHAPTER FIFTY-EIGHT

Tuesday, 15 October 2013

While Livermore and Nottage were in conference, Grace checked out the messages on her mobile.

The first was a text from Ross Yardley. It read, "You cost me almost £1,000 to repair my bonnet. I'd like to say 'no hard feelings', but I get them in my trousers every time I think about you.'

She texted him a one-word reply: "Arsehole."

The second message was from her father, telling her that there was no improvement in her mother's condition. There was a risk that her infection would get worse and she might have to undergo an operation.

Grace felt a mixture of concern and guilt – she must fly to Senegal soon.

But the third message on her phone brought her mind back to the murder enquiry. It was from Pixie Whitechurch, informing Grace that she'd spent part of the previous night with a man called Rick. She'd agreed to provide 'extras', and his sexual preferences made it clear he was the 'oddball' to whom Zena – alias Anna Marie – had been referring.

Pixie had learned that Rick was just his nickname. His full name was Kendrick Alleyne, and the address the club had for him was 112 Ruskin House on the outskirts of Brighton.

Conteh discussed the situation with O'Sullivan and Dimbleby. "Leave it with us," said O'Sullivan. "The chief asked us to chase it up, and that's what we'll do. We'll pay Mr Alleyne a visit."

Before Conteh could argue that Pixie was her contact and therefore she should check out Rick with Nottage, her mobile sounded. She looked at the text, thinking it may have been Pixie again, but it was another call from Ross. This one read, 'When you say 'arsehole', is that the next erogenous zone you want me to explore?'

Flushing with embarrassment and anger, she sent him another one-word reply: "Bastard!"

In the brief time that she'd been distracted, O'Sullivan and Dimbleby had departed.

CHAPTER FIFTY-NINE

Tuesday, 15 October 2013

"What a dump!" said Dimbleby as he and O'Sullivan pulled into a litter-strewn parking lot at the council housing estate where Kendrick Alleyne resided.

Virtually all the walls adjoining the flats were covered in graffiti, and there was a pool of urine in the lift servicing Ruskin House. The smell was so bad that they opted to climb the stairs to the fourth floor, passing three youngsters rushing down at such a pace they almost knocked the two men over.

When they got to No. 112 Ruskin House, O'Sullivan pushed on a doorbell that didn't seem to work and resorted to knocking hard on a grimy door from which some of the blue paint was peeling badly.

"Hold on, Harry," shouted a gruff Afro-Caribbean voice from inside. "Give me a bloody chance. I've got the stuff for you."

The black man who threw the door open was a six-foot-five-inch colossus with granite-like features and Afro hair. His appearance seemed to be influenced greatly by eccentric pop star Prince because, in addition to the frizzy hairdo, he had an ostentatious ear cuff and large, gaudy sunglasses.

This giant in yellow pants and matching high-heeled boots appeared to be even more shocked to see them than the policemen were to clock his appearance.

"And what stuff would that be?" asked Dimbleby.

"Who the fucking hell are you?"

"Are you Kendrick Alleyne?" O'Sullivan interjected.

"What if I am?"

"We're police officers, sir," said O'Sullivan, showing him his warrant card. "Now, as my colleague asked, what was that stuff you were talking about when you thought we were Harry?"

The giant attempted to slam the door shut, but O'Sullivan had already moved forward and forced it open again.

Alleyne's swift reaction took the policemen by surprise. Showing speed that belied his enormous size, he lashed out with his fist. The blow was so accurately and viciously delivered that it split O'Sullivan's nose.

The detective sergeant staggered back, groaning and clutching his wound, with blood pouring over his face.

As O'Sullivan crumbled to the floor, Alleyne climbed over him, evaded Dimbleby's attempt to grab him, and did a runner.

Dimbleby gave chase, but the much younger, more powerful man was too fast for him, and by the time the police officer reached the parking lot, Alleyne was already reviving up his car, a black BMW.

The out-of-breath copper was able to get the registration number, however, and put out a police alert to have it stopped.

When Dimbleby got back to the flat, he found O'Sullivan inside the kitchen washing the blood from his nose and then holding a handkerchief over the open wound.

The untidy flat was decked out with a massive flat-screen television and a range of mod cons, including a PlayStation, iPads, and two laptops. On the lounge table was a large package, bound with adhesive tape.

"It seems chummy was about to hand over some drugs," said Dimbleby, going over to the package and prising part of it open to reveal white powder wrapped in cellophane.

"Looks like cocaine. We called at the worst possible time as far as Mr Alleyne was concerned."

"Obviously we did. But the man was a fool to punch me and run out of his own flat," moaned O'Sullivan, still dabbing his nose gingerly. "We can now charge him with assaulting a police officer and dealing in drugs before we even get to his possible involvement with the murder of Zena Cattermole."

"Too right, Mike. He drove off like a bat out of hell, but he won't get far. I've given out his registration number, so he should soon be picked up. Shall we look around this shithole?"

"Let's do it."

They moved into the bedroom where they were confronted with a large black and white photograph on the wall of a naked woman, gagged and bound to a chair by chains.

"It appears our friend Alleyne was into bondage. There's. . ."

O'Sullivan was interrupted by a knock on the front door. "That will no doubt be Harry," said Dimbleby in a whisper. "I'm pretty good at voices, so why don't I impersonate Alleyne?"

The knock on the front door was repeated.

"OK, OK," shouted Dimbleby in his best attempt at an Afro-Caribbean accent. "Is that you Harry?"

"Yeah, sorry I'm a bit late, mate. Are you going to let me in or what?"

"You caught me taking a piss," Dimbleby informed the man by way of explanation. "Hold on, I'm just coming. I've got the crack for you. Have you got the cash?"

"Yeah, it's all here. Now bloody well let me in, Rick."

Dimbleby obliged and promptly arrested the startled man.

CHAPTER SIXTY

Tuesday, 15 October 2013

The unfortunate O'Sullivan had insult added to his physical injury by his colleagues' cruel jibes.

"You've clearly got a nose for this police work," said Nottage when the Irishman returned to the office nursing his disfigured hooter. There were roars of laughter from Dimbleby, Conteh, and Yedding until O'Sullivan glared at them.

"Very funny," he moaned. "I'd have expected better from you, Jeff. Come to think of it, I suppose I wouldn't."

"Sorry," Nottage said by way of a mock apology. "But there's a lesson we can all learn from this."

"Which is?" growled O'Sullivan, falling into the trap that had been set for him by his mischievous colleague.

"Don't poke your nose in where it isn't wanted." More laughter followed.

"Sod you all. If that's how you feel, I'm going to get some first aid instead of sitting here listening to abuse." With that, O'Sullivan stormed out of the room.

"Talk about kicking a man when he's down," muttered Dimbleby. It was hard to make out whether he was joking or complaining on behalf of his partner. "This is the second time poor old Mike has been assaulted. He was thumped by another suspect a few weeks back."

"We'll have to nickname him Mr A & E," said Nottage unsympathetically. "Now, if you'll excuse us, Conteh and I have to go and interview a witness."

*****

When the two of them were in the car on the way to visiting the chairman of Anderida Writers, Nottage again had a chuckle. "I can't get over O'Sullivan having his nose bashed in. It's poetic justice."

"Yes, he can be annoying sometimes. But you were a bit hard on him, don't you think?"

"Not at all. He's dished out enough snide remarks in the past, and a lot of them have been directed at me. As I told you before, he obviously resents the fact I was made up to DI instead of him. This time it was my turn to be the clever Dick."

Conteh gave him a disapproving look.

"Obviously you think I went too far. My wife would no doubt agree with you if she'd been there. She says I've a habit of putting into words what other people are thinking but unwilling to say. I call that being honest. But perhaps I'm too outspoken."

"I'm glad you're outspoken, Jeff. You kindly stuck up for me when I was getting a dressing down from DCI Livermore. I'm sure it was your intervention that prevented me being thrown off the case, and I appreciate it very much. But perhaps it would've been better if I'd been suspended."

"That's a strange thing to say, Grace."

"My mother is seriously ill in hospital in Senegal. If I wasn't still part of the murder investigation team, I'd have flown out to visit her."

"Why haven't you asked for compassionate leave?"

"I didn't feel that would be appropriate after my relationship with Yardley backfired so spectacularly."

"You can't keep beating yourself up about that. When we get back to the office, I'll square it with Livermore for you to take immediate leave. One phone call from him to Fussy Frampton should do the trick. You'd never forgive yourself if your mother died and you weren't with her."

"Thank you, Jeff. Thank you so much." She leaned over and kissed him on the cheek. "About what you were saying earlier . . ., may I make an observation?"

"Go ahead."

"Honesty is obviously a fine quality, but I find that it pays not to be too blunt. It's usually a good idea to include a few words of sympathy or appreciation when dishing out stick."

"Good point. I'll take your advice on board and try to be Mr Nice Guy."

Nottage had the ideal opportunity to show his kinder, more patient side when they spoke to the Anderida chairman Tony Flood, a rotund, colourfully dressed, exuberant man who insisted they sit on the balcony of his town house to enjoy the harbour view.

Before they could ask their questions, he told them, "My wife and I love Sovereign Harbour. It's one of Europe's largest marina complexes, with four linked harbours and over 3,000 properties."

He then announced he was going into the kitchen to bring them tea and biscuits.

Nottage couldn't resist making a sarcastic remark to Conteh. "Does he think we want to buy the place?"

Their host obviously heard this jibe, despite being in the kitchen, and called out, "The houses on the right are called Millionaire's Row, so they would be out of your price range – and mine. Their yacht berths alone cost around £50,000. Excuse me while I go downstairs to get some milk from our fridge."

Nottage rolled his eyes and took the opportunity to let off steam. "He obviously thinks he's smart and he's right – he's a smart-arse!"

"He's just being friendly. Don't forget you promised to be nice."

"OK, OK."

Upon returning, Flood arranged a small table in front of his visitors and served them tea in Wedgwood cups.

"I understand you've written books yourself, Mr Flood," the detective inspector said as he dipped his biscuit into his drink. "Anything . . ."

"Yes," said their host, not needing any encouragement to talk about himself. "I've dabbled in two or three genres, including writing a celebrity book called 'My Life With the Stars' containing revelations about famous personalities I interviewed when I was a journalist and Sky Television executive."

"Can't say I've come across it, sir," commented Nottage, reverting to his more acerbic style, which brought him another of Conteh's disapproving looks.

The inspector got down to business by explaining how two of the Anderida members had recalled seeing Monty Remington at the writing group's last meeting.

"Yes, he was there."

"But was he present throughout the meeting? Did he arrive late or leave early?"

Flood's brow furrowed as he searched his memory. "He was late."

"Are you sure?"

"Quite sure, Inspector. I was sitting at the top table, facing the members and right in line with the entrance to the room in which we were meeting. Monty sneaked in shortly before the interval."

"That's interesting," said Nottage. "The two members we spoke to didn't recall that."

"What did they tell you?"

"One of them, Dorothy Hardcastle, remembers talking to Monty during the interval at 9 p.m.," Conteh volunteered.

"Ah, dear Dotty. She seems to have lived up to her name and got slightly muddled. I think the time she's given you is incorrect."

"How can that be?" queried Nottage.

"She may've got confused because we do usually break at 9 p.m., but the speaker overran that night. By the time we'd asked questions, it was probably nearer 9.30 when we broke for tea and coffee."

"So what time do you think Monty turned up?" Conteh asked.

"Probably five minutes before the interval. So that would've been around 9.25. Does it make much difference?"

"Yes, it could put a different complexion on things," Nottage revealed. "Did Monty seem his usual self?"

"Yes, I think so, but I only spoke to him briefly. Why do you ask?"

"Are you aware that Monty has an identical twin brother?" Conteh said, answering his question with another.

"No, I wasn't – and there was I thinking that Monty, like me, must be a one-off," the extrovert writing group chairman chuckled.

"Could it have been his twin brother Justin who was at your meeting and not Monty?" Conteh suggested.

"I don't think so – but I can't be certain. Is it important?"

"Very important," emphasised Nottage. "It's in connection with a murder investigation."

"Hmm. I'd like to be able to come up with some masterstroke of detection for you, such as saying I spotted that Mr Remington drank coffee when he normally has tea, but I didn't notice anything unusual about him."

"Never mind," Conteh assured the man. "You've been a great help with the timings you've given us."

While showing them out, the author picked up one of his books from a large pile and gave it to the policewoman. "I think these showbiz and sports anecdotes will appeal to you." Then, almost as an afterthought, he added, "There's one other thing that might interest you."

"I'm not much of a reader," said Nottage, without breaking step.

"I was going to give you another piece of information, not a book," Flood rebuked mildly. "It may help you to know that Monty Remington has been researching for a thriller he's writing about a serial killer."

*****

Back in the car, Nottage and Conteh could hardly contain their excitement.

"Well, well, well," chortled the delighted inspector. "Now we know that whichever twin was at the Anderida meeting didn't arrive there until just before 9.30. Monty would've had time to commit the murder in Brighton at around 8.30 p.m. and get to Eastbourne an hour later."

"But how would he have cleaned himself up?"

"Good point, Grace."

"So perhaps my theory was right that one twin impersonated the other. Monty could have committed the murder and then phoned Justin, asking him to attend the Anderida meeting in his place to give him an alibi."

"That would explain it. What could be significant is that Monty has been writing a book on serial killers – perhaps he was plotting the murders under the guise of doing research."

Conteh nodded. "But we also have another suspect in Kendrick Alleyne. It will be interesting to see what he's got to say for himself when we catch up with him."

CHAPTER SIXTY-ONE

Wednesday, 16 October 2013

Within twenty-four hours Grace was on her way to Senegal – and Kendrick Alleyne had been arrested. Shortly before midday on Wednesday he was being questioned under caution by Nottage and Dimbleby in the interview room.

The arrogant thirty-five-year-old, built like a heavyweight wrestler whose muscular upper body was threatening to burst out of his sweatshirt, simply said "no comment" to everything that was put to him.

Nottage suspended the interview so that Alleyne could take a toilet break. Before it was resumed, he suggested to Alleyne that it might be in his interest to answer their questions.

"You can both go to hell!"

"If we did, we'd probably bump into you again," retorted Dimbleby.

Nottage gave Dimbleby a warning glare before switching on the recording equipment and announcing that the interview was resuming.

"So far, Mr Alleyne, you have answered 'no comment' to every question. Is there anything you do want to tell us?"

"No – I've got nothing to say to you bastards."

"It's up to you. But you might want to explain to us what you were doing at the time of the murder."

"I ain't committed any fucking murder," the African-American shouted, rising abruptly from his stiff-backed seat and knocking it over.

"Go steady with the furniture," Dimbleby chided.

"You said you didn't want a solicitor," Nottage reminded their new suspect. "But would you like one now?"

"Why should I need a solicitor?" asked Alleyne, picking up the chair and sitting in it again. "There's no way you can pin this woman's murder on me. I don't even know who she is."

"It's already been explained to you that the lady we've been asking you about was Zena Cattermole. You knew her as a dancer called Anna Marie at the Krazy Knights nightclub where you're a member. You went to a hotel and had sex with her, didn't you?"

"Prove it," challenged the enraged Alleyne, eyeballing the inspector.

"That won't be hard. Your nickname 'Rick' is in her diary, in which she's written beside it 'paid £120'. And she told a friend about how she gave you a few 'extras'."

"OK, so what?"

"How many times did you go to a hotel with her?"

"Twice."

"Why only twice? Didn't she meet your requirements?"

"She was a great lay, man. It you must know, she blew my head away."

"So you wanted more. You went around to her flat on Monday last week and made further demands on her. When she wouldn't oblige, you killed her."

"That's a load of fucking rubbish!" shouted Alleyne, leaning over the interview table and glaring at the two officers facing him. "You're trying to fit me up."

"We know you're into bondage," said Dimbleby, unperturbed. "The magazines and videos we found in your flat prove that. You like to see women tied in chains, rope, handcuffs, and bondage tape. Gives you a thrill, doesn't it? Perhaps you wanted to perform certain sexual acts on Anna Marie which she wouldn't agree to. So you got in a rage and murdered her."

"Hell, that doesn't make any sense at all, man."

"To a drug-taker like you, things don't have to make sense," Nottage pointed out. "We know you've been peddling crack. Not only was a package of cocaine found in your flat, but your mate Harry admits that you were about to sell it to him."

"OK, so I was going to let him have some coke as a favour."

"We also found heroin in your flat. And the puncture marks on your arms show that you're taking drugs yourself. That can result in paranoid thinking, nausea, severe agitation, and hallucinations. You're capable of all kinds of irrational acts as you demonstrated when you broke the nose of one of my officers."

"This is a bloody stitch-up. I've nothing more to say – nothing at all. Now can I go?"

"Are you joking?" Dimbleby derided.

"No, you can't go," confirmed Nottage. "We'll be seeking an extension to hold you in custody."

"You can't do that, man. I've got my rights."

"And we've got ours, Mr Alleyne. You may recall that when you were last arrested on a drugs related matter two years ago, you broke the terms of your bail by intimidating one of the witnesses. So you'll be sitting in a police cell overnight. And it remains to be seen whether a charge of murder will be added to those of assaulting a police officer and possessing drugs with the intent to supply."

CHAPTER SIXTY-TWO

Thursday, 17 October 2013

The next day Kendrick Alleyne was ready to talk to them about the woman he'd known as Anna Marie, but his manner hadn't changed. He was belligerent, aggressive, and cocksure – so much so that he again refused to request a solicitor be in the interview room with him.

"I've admitted I had a couple of sessions with the tart in a hotel, but I never went to her flat. I didn't even know where she lived. I didn't kill her, man. Don't go trying to pin that on me."

"Presumably you first met her in her role as a dancer," said Nottage calmly.

"Yeah. She did a lap dance and came on to me. So I went with her to a hotel afterwards. But all this was weeks ago."

"You paid her for sex twice?" Dimbleby clarified, his face betraying the trace of a smile.

Alleyne refused to answer. Instead, he simply glared at them.

"What's the matter? Are you ashamed to admit it?" Dimbleby prompted.

Alleyne clammed up completely and sat there twiddling his large thumbs.

"You dress like Prince, but you don't act like him. Just because you share his birthplace of Minneapolis doesn't mean you have his style."

"Leave him out of this!" Alleyne hissed, his brown eyes blazing.

"Yes, it was amiss of me," admitted Dimbleby. "A superstar like Prince would never pay for sex. But, in fairness, you don't have his pulling power. So there's no shame in admitting it."

"OK, I bloody well paid her – that's no crime, is it?"

"It is if you cut her with your knife and killed her," said Nottage.

"I didn't do nothing to her!" stormed Alleyne, rising to his feet menacingly.

"Please sit down, Mr Alleyne," Nottage advised. "You're in enough trouble already for assaulting a police officer and peddling drugs." The DI refused to be intimidated by Alleyne's piercing glare, and after a few seconds, the big man resumed sitting.

"So what did happen?" asked Nottage. "Did you want to perform certain sexual acts on Anna Marie and she refused to let you?"

"No way."

"Things got out of hand, didn't they?"

"It wasn't like that."

"What was it like then? You asked her to indulge in a spot of bondage, did you?"

"You've got it all wrong, man. Just because I've got bondage magazines and videos doesn't mean I go around tying up women or gagging them."

"So what did you get up to with Anna Marie?"

Alleyne sighed. "She did a private striptease for me, let me touch her, and then we had sex. There was no bondage. And I didn't cut her, man."

"But you do have a knife," Dimbleby pointed out. "We discovered it in your flat."

"Hell, so I own a knife, but I didn't even have it on me when I was with her."

"We're having it examined," Dimbleby told him. "When we get the results, we'll know if you're telling the truth. Meanwhile, where do you claim you were on the night of Monday, October 7th?"

Alleyne appeared to give it some thought but came up with nothing. "I don't know, man. I was probably spaced out."

"Well," said Nottage almost sympathetically, "things are looking bad for you. You admit having sex with the murder victim, you own a knife similar to the weapon that killed her, and you don't have an alibi."

*****

"What do you think, Gov?" asked Nottage, after joining Livermore in his office. "Is Alleyne the killer?"

272

"He could be," Livermore answered, rubbing his fingers across the stubble on his chin. "We've seen how out of control he gets when he loses his temper – O'Sullivan has been on the receiving end of it. So Alleyne would've been quite likely to lose his rag if the promiscuous Anna Marie reverted to the prim and proper Zena Cattermole, and didn't agree to what he wanted. Should his knife have any traces of her blood on it, then we've got our man. But, if it doesn't, we could be left with the fact that he simply can't account for where he was on the night of the murder.

"So far we have no actual evidence, and we're going to have to let him go on bail."

Nottage sighed. "That brings us back to Monty Remington."

"It does indeed. Monty's alibi no longer stands up, and as you pointed out, forensic evidence could show he was with Zena. The problem is the dark brown hairs we found on her dress could match either of the twins."

CHAPTER SIXTY-THREE

Friday, 18 October 2013

He was fully focused on the latest news item on TV concerning the murder of Zena Cattermole.

Despite again being consumed by a feeling of dissatisfaction, he couldn't resist chuckling when the newsreader said that police had interviewed two men who would be continuing to help them with their enquiries. "They don't know a bloody thing," he said to himself.

But he reflected sadly that the last of his three victims had literally run out on him. And he cursed when the newsreader referred to her as a nightclub lap dancer.

"That's it, you bastard – rub it in that I couldn't even make it with a fucking tart!" he shouted at the screen as he rammed his forefinger into the 'off' button and hurled the remote control across the room.

She should've been willing to have rough sex with him. But, instead, the silly bitch had kneed him in the groin and done a runner after he'd told her exactly what he intended to do to her.

On reflection, his lack of subtlety had been a huge mistake, but, as with the two previous victims, 'Mr Hyde' had taken over and he'd been completely consumed by lust.

Of course, the voices in his head were to blame. These demons had driven him to taking drugs, committing acts of violence and far worse.

'Loser,' chided a voice that sounded just like his stepmother's.

"Shut up, shut up!" he shouted.

Why wouldn't the bloody demons go away?

This latest experience had left him furious and even more sexually frustrated. Now the feelings of anger and being unfulfilled were becoming even stronger.

He needed a woman oozing sex appeal who would fully succumb to his demands – and he knew the very one. This time he would not be rejected and made to feel inadequate.

CHAPTER SIXTY-FOUR

Saturday, 19 October 2013

Nottage liked the occasional bet and made a point of studying the odds. But he didn't have to be an expert to know those on Alleyne being the murderer had shortened considerably when it came to light that he had been seen harassing Anna Marie.

The questioning of Krazy Knights members had finally paid off, with one of them, an old rake called Nathan Jamieson, recalling seeing Alleyne confront her outside the club a few days before she was killed.

Nottage was quick to pass on this new information to his boss. "Mr Jamieson told one of our team that Alleyne had blocked Anna Marie's path as she was leaving and called her a bitch.

"She had to push her way past him and jump into a taxi which was waiting for her," Nottage reported. "Alleyne shouted after her. Jamieson said he heard him make a threatening remark – something about making her pay."

Livermore's face lit up. "It seems Alleyne has been lying to us all along. This confrontation with Zena suggests she no longer wanted anything to do with him and really pissed him off."

"It really puts a different complexion on things, doesn't it, Gov?"

"Yes, and talking about complexions, Alleyne's skin colour is so pale that, from a distance, he could be mistaken for a white man. So the bloke seen on CCTV wearing a hat and approaching Zena's flat on the night of the murder could have been him."

Nottage concurred. "That makes sense, Gov. He must have been furious with Zena when she snubbed him outside the nightclub – perhaps furious enough to go to her flat and teach her a lesson."

"That's what we need to find out, Jeff. Alleyne's time on bail is about to come to an abrupt end. Go out and arrest him again!"

CHAPTER SIXTY-FIVE

Saturday, 19 October 2013

Katrina stretched out on the studio couch in her flat, wearing a red kimono and not much else while she checked some of the sketches drawn by her art students.

It was a dull Saturday morning, but she'd been enjoying her own company – and that of her adorable tabby kitten Jezebel, who'd just jumped on to her lap. The cat purred loudly at having its soft fur stroked.

When the doorbell rang, Jezebel took fright as usual, scuttling off into the kitchen.

"Who is it?" Katrina called, going towards the door.

"It's me, Justin."

She let him in and gave him a kiss on the cheek.

"What brings you here?"

"I was passing and thought I'd drop in. I hope it's not an inconvenient time."

"No. As you can see, I'm chilling out," she assured him, referring to her casual attire.

She made some coffee, and they sat drinking it on the stylish upholstered couch. But their conversation was stilted.

"You look good," he muttered and reached out to stroke her soft pink cheek. His fingers continued their downward path, brushing her neck and then the outline of her left breast through the soft silk of her loose-fitting Japanese robe. She wasn't wearing a bra, and he was able to rub her clearly visible nipple.

It felt distinctly like a grope, so she brushed his hand away.

"Not in the mood, eh?" he grunted. "Or is it me?"

Katrina had never felt like this in his company before, and there seemed to be a hint of aggression in his demeanour as he stared at her.

"What's the matter with you, Justin?" She went cold as she noticed he'd draped a scarf over the back of the couch. "You are Justin, aren't you?"

"Why do you say that?"

"Because you were wearing a scarf. You told me you didn't like scarves." She got up startled as the penny dropped. "Good grief, you're not Justin, are you? You're Monty."

"No, I'm not Monty," he stressed, rising to his feet. "I'm Victor."

"Victor? Who the devil are you?"

"Victor – Justin's other brother."

"But you're the spitting image of him – you must be Monty. Otherwise, how is that possible?"

"Because, Miss Clever Dick, we're identical TRIPLETS."

"Triplets aren't identical."

"Some are. We're a rarity – one in a million."

"Justin has never said anything about you."

"That's because I shouldn't think either he or Monty have a clue I even exist."

Katrina was frightened but also perplexed. "How so?"

"Finally someone's taking an interest in me! Apparently, our loving mother was very ill after giving birth to us. She was unmarried and broke, so it was decided that one of us had to be given away. I was the unlucky one.

"I was offloaded on a depraved couple, whose idea of fun was to sexually assault me when they got fed up with fucking each other. My backside was so sore I couldn't sit down at times. The only thing they ever gave me was a cat, and they said they'd slit its throat if I ever told anyone they were buggering me senseless. The sod who called himself my father would point to his knife hanging in a sheath on the wall to remind me.

"One day the old bastard caught me trying to phone a helpline. He grabbed hold of my cat and hacked off its tail."

Victor's voice cracked, and it was obvious that the memories were distressing him. "They never told me about my real mother or that I had any brothers until I was ten – and then one day they just blurted it all out. My dear stepfather – who I affectionately called the Robot – said my real mother kept her best two bastards and gave me away because she hated the sight of me."

"How dreadful! I'm sorry."

"It's my step-parents you should feel sorry for. I celebrated my eighteenth birthday by giving them a taste of their own medicine. They screamed for mercy until I finally put them out of their misery. But that's enough about me! It's time you and I had some fun together."

His smirk sent a cold shiver through her. "You must be joking," she said, feeling nauseous and pulling the kimono more tightly around her body in a defensive gesture. "I want you to leave right now."

"I don't think so," Victor replied coldly, invading her space. He opened his coat, revealing a belt, to which was attached a metal sheath. From it he withdrew a large commando-style knife.

"What do you think of this? It's got a metal hilt and wooden handle just like the Robot used to have."

Although she was gripped with fear, Katrina felt she had to keep him talking to buy herself time as she backed away. "How did you know where to find me?"

"Aren't you the inquisitive one? I simply popped into the dating agency and pretended I was Justin. I said I'd mislaid the details they'd sent me, so they gave me a copy which contained your name and phone number. I looked up your address in the telephone directory, just as I'd done with a lady in Brighton, who unfortunately is no longer with us."

Katrina became aware that when this man was in full flow, he spat his words out far too quickly – he wasn't talking to her but at her.

"How did you find out that Justin belonged to the agency?"

Victor began to run his forefinger menacingly around the tip of the knife. She watched in horror, sensing that he was growing impatient, but he answered her question. "I didn't know anything about Justin until I read in the local paper that he'd taken over some investment company. There was a picture of him in his plush expensive flat, so I decided to break in and relieve him of some of his valuables. While I was there, I also took a brochure he'd received from the dating agency. He'd been helpful enough to tick some of the talent on show." ·

"So you contacted the women he'd already met, making out you were Justin."

"You've got it. You're a regular little Miss Marple, aren't you? Unfortunately, the three ladies I picked out didn't seem to fancy me. They obviously felt I wasn't as charming as they'd remembered when they were actually with my dear brother Justin. They refused to play ball, so I had to take what I wanted from them by force."

"And then you killed them."

"It was their own bloody stupid faults. The first two silly cows became hysterical, and the third ran out screaming. It didn't have to end that way. If they hadn't rejected my advances, I wouldn't have had to knife them. Now you've got the same choice."

Victor twisted the knife handle in his right hand, causing the double-sided blade to shine in the light from the window.

As they stared at each other, Katrina could see that, despite Victor's uncanny likeness to Justin, there were some differences. His red watery eyes and puffy cheeks, coupled with his excessive talkativeness, were the telltale signs of drug abuse. And his threatening manner was frightening.

"So are you going to cooperate, or shall I use the knife on you?"

Katrina decided to pretend she'd go along with what he wanted. She forced herself to smile at him even though the glare from his piercing eyes sent a chill right through her.

"When you put it like that, I think I suddenly feel in the mood for sex."

"Good. Put on those red shoes," he ordered, pointing to her high heels that lay beside the sofa.

Katrina slipped her small feet into them. *'It's time to use another teasing routine. It's the only way to stop him from killing me.'*

"Do you like me in heels?" she cooed, twirling provocatively so that her kimono rose and he could admire her legs. "Let's go to the bedroom, shall we?"

He hesitated, and she knew she had to seize the initiative. "Now are you all talk, or have you got something inside your trousers that might interest me?"

He grinned and put the knife back in its sheath as she provocatively led the way.

Once in the bedroom, Katrina gently rubbed the front of his trousers. It didn't achieve quite the response she anticipated, but, undeterred, she started to undo his belt, causing his trousers to slip around his ankles.

Victor slid his hands up the back of her legs inside her kimono. His fingers moved over her thighs and firmly gripped her shapely buttocks. He squeezed her bottom cheeks tightly and then tugged at her skimpy black bikini briefs. "You won't need these," he said, yanking at them until they slid down her legs and dropped to the floor.

Revulsion came over her in waves, but she forced herself to act as a temptress. Katrina brushed his unshaven cheek with her lips and pressed her body against his. She then moved her right hand over the bulge she'd finally created and eased Victor's penis gently through the slit in his boxer pants. It wasn't anywhere near as big as Katrina had expected, but increased in size as she teased it with her fingers.

His thumbs were pressing into her bum. And when he eased the pressure, it was simply to move two of his fingers towards an area where no man had ever been allowed to enter.

She tried desperately not to show her disgust. "Just what have you got in mind, Victor?"

"Anal," he replied curtly. "Don't worry. I won't use the knife on you. My long metal sheath will do the trick. But that's something for you to look forward to after I've fucked you."

Katrina's mind was racing. *I have to play along and keep speaking to distract this disgusting pig.*

"Aren't a lucky girl? But first things first – we've got to make sure your cock is nice and hard, haven't we?"

She continued stroking it, and then knelt down so that her tongue ran along its full length. When Victor's tool became stiffer, she kissed the tip of it.

He gasped as she took him in her month. But she'd no sooner done so than she sunk her teeth deep into the penis, biting it as hard as she could.

He yelled in agony, and blood seeped from his injured weapon. "You bitch!" he cried out, pushing her away and grasping the wound. "You'll pay for that."

But Katrina was already on her feet and moving rapidly across to her wardrobe. She flung open the door and removed a shoebox from the top shelf. Frantically she tugged the lid off.

Victor stumbled towards her, his bleeding penis hanging limply out of his pants, and his trousers down around his ankles. But the most noticeable thing about him was that he now had the knife in his hand.

He lunged forward, his eyes blazing with anger, obviously intent on making Katrina his fourth victim.

But he was taken completely by surprise as a startled Jezebel raced into the room. The scatty kitten dived between Victor's legs, causing him to lose balance and trip over his own trousers.

It gave Katrina the vital few extra seconds she needed. Fumbling in the shoebox, she pulled out her gun. "Get back, you bastard!" she shouted, having to hold the snub-nosed revolver in both hands because she was shaking.

"You won't use that," Victor scoffed, climbing to his feet and moving menacingly forward with the knife blade flashing as she backed away. "You haven't got the guts."

"You're the second man to say that to me – and the first one is no longer alive."

He showed no sign of heeding the warning, so she pulled the trigger!

CHAPTER SIXTY-SIX

Monday, 21 October 2013

"So," Nottage said, taking a seat in Livermore's office, "nobody will be shedding any tears over the death of Victor Remington. Who'd have thought the murderer would turn out to be an identical triplet hardly anyone knew existed?"

"Yes, most unusual. But it's still alarming that we had no records about Victor – or even that Justin's brother Monty was a twin, let alone a triplet."

Nottage was quick to provide an excuse for the oversight by his colleagues. "There was a good reason for it, Gov. As I explained to you previously, Justin was born on December 31st, 1981, but Monty was delivered a couple of hours later on the first day of 1982. Victor came into the world after Monty, so these two were both born in a different year to Justin.

"The admin error which resulted in Monty's birth date being entered on our files as the eleventh month instead of the first month didn't give any indication that we were dealing with twins or triplets. To add to the confusion, Victor was given to foster parents."

Livermore leaned back in his chair and shook his head. "But why wasn't Victor on our records at all? It's easy to understand that as their mother was unmarried, in poor health, and probably had money problems, she couldn't bring up three boys. That explains why she gave Victor away, but it must've been documented."

"Apparently not," Nottage corrected. "He was never entered by his mother on a birth certificate – instead, the couple who adopted him registered him as their own son. He was given their surname, so throughout his life he was known as Victor Hobbs."

Livermore again shook his head in frustration. "Not knowing about the triplets doesn't put us in a good light. Goodness knows what Fussy Frampton will say to me when he finally stops giving press interviews."

"You might like to point out to him that identical triplets occur only once in between 100 to 200 million births."

"That's not a very precise figure, Jeff."

"I checked with a specialist, Gov, and cases of identical triplets happen so infrequently that it's difficult to come up with exact statistics. It's amazing, isn't it, that a single fertilised egg splits and becomes three different embryos? The odds of three babies developing and surviving from one egg are astronomical."

Nottage put on his spectacles to refer to his case notes. "A woman from Pontypool gave birth to a set of identical girl triplets this year. The three babies were born two months early and were in intensive care for six weeks. They were so small that they had a combined weight of less than eleven pounds at birth, and all three could be held in one hand. The Remingtons were healthier babies, but there's always a risk. As the third arrival, Victor might not have survived."

"It's a bloody pity he did. If he'd died at birth, then those three women wouldn't have been murdered."

Nottage nodded. "It's a bit puzzling how all three boys developed such different personalities. I thought identical triplets not only shared the exact same features but the same characteristics too. I suppose life's experiences can drastically change people."

"You seem to have answered your own question." Livermore ran his hand over his stubbly chin as he gave the matter further consideration. "If events occur that are traumatic during a person's upbringing and lifetime, then they're bound to affect them – sometimes dramatically.

"Our serial killer was labelled a psychopath, but Victor's condition was probably more complex – perhaps he was schizophrenic with sociopathic tendencies. Sociopathy is likely the result of childhood trauma and physical or emotional abuse. That might explain the differences between him and his brothers.

"We don't know why Monty is homosexual and Justin heterosexual, but we're now aware of events that caused Victor to become so bitter, twisted, and perverted. Whereas Justin and Monty appear to have had happy childhoods, Victor certainly did not.

"According to what he told Katrina Merton, he was regularly sexually assaulted by his foster parents. I'm no psychologist, but that obviously had a huge effect on Victor. Imagine what a bitter blow it must've been for him to then find out, as a teenager, that the depraved couple who'd raised him weren't his real parents – and that he had two brothers who'd been brought up normally!"

"Yeah, it must have messed with his head. But the killings came much later, Gov."

"The final straw for Victor was probably seeing a picture of his brother Justin in a newspaper article and realising how affluent he was. No doubt Victor became deeply jealous and resentful of Justin even though he'd never met him."

"That doesn't fully explain why he resorted to murdering those three women or even why he targeted them in the first place," Nottage pointed out.

"It's reasonable to believe that he broke into Justin's flat to rob him as an act of vengeance. While doing so, he came across Justin's dating agency brochure and thought it would be the perfect way to find 'foxy' females.

"When Victor pretended to be Justin and called on three of the women his brother had already met, he presumably assumed they would consent to have sex with him. But, instead, they rejected him. So he raped and murdered them."

"That wraps it up then," Nottage concurred. "And it lets Justin, Monty, Carl Tarbutt, and Kendrick Alleyne off the hook – but now we have to deal with Katrina Merton."

"Quite so," sighed Livermore.

"You were first to arrive at the crime scene, Gov, and the rest of us never got to talk to her, as we were tracking down Kendrick Alleyne. What did you make of her explanation?"

"She simply told me how Victor had tried to pose as Justin but then admitted he was his brother and threatened her with a knife. She was in no state to explain exactly how she turned the tables on him. The experience left her traumatised, and she's still being treated for shock. I'll leave it a couple of days before I formally interview her."

CHAPTER SIXTY-SEVEN

Tuesday, 22 October 2013

Grace Conteh was in tears as she slumped exhausted into a chair in the corridor outside a private ward in Dakar's Principal Hospital.

When she'd arrived in this sunshine city, she'd been told that her mother was near to death and needed an operation. Since then Grace had hardly slept and now felt shattered.

She didn't notice her father returning after visiting the canteen. He crouched in front of her and gently touched her knee. "What's the matter, Grace? Is it bad news? Has she passed away?"

"No, it's good news, Dad. The doctor has just seen me and told me that Mum is making satisfactory progress following her op."

"Thank heavens for that. When I saw you sobbing, I feared the worst."

"They're tears of joy, not sorrow," she blurted out, forcing a smile that masked how her deepest fears were being replaced by intense relief.

"So why are you sitting out here? Why aren't you at your mother's bedside?"

"She's still asleep – she hasn't woken since you went to grab something to eat. But the doctor says he's confident the operation has been successful. I'm so tired myself I flopped into this chair after talking to him. If I'd tried to stay on my feet, I'd probably have fallen flat on my face. But I'm also extremely relieved and happy – Mum's going to be OK."

CHAPTER SIXTY-EIGHT

Tuesday, 22 October 2013

Livermore had instructed his team to find out as much about Victor Remington as they could under his registered name of Victor Hobbs, and on Tuesday afternoon they reported back to him.

Nottage informed those gathered in the incident room that Hobbs had learned how to use a knife during his service with the British Armed Forces in Afghanistan.

"I've spoken to his former commanding officer, and he provided an insight that suggests Hobbs had a lust for violence. He was given the nickname 'Rambo', and apparently it was well earned because he saw himself as a warrior. Victor had a love of knives and guns, and following an incident in which he injured one of his own men, he was discharged before completing a tour of duty."

O'Sullivan, who was sitting on a desktop as usual but with a plaster over his nose and his breath emitting the smell of a liquid lunch, for once fully supported Nottage. "That fits in with what I've found out about his civilian life. He was a bit of a recluse and was self-employed, repairing computers, but belonged to a gun club where he failed to abide by their code of conduct and had his membership terminated.

"The search of his flat uncovered a couple of guns and several knives, plus books on weapons and violence. There was also a big collection of mags and DVDs, mostly pornographic, but they included the Rambo films. He even borrowed books on Rambo from Eastbourne Library.

"The most interesting thing we came across in his flat was a pair of size 11 shoes with leather soles. They'd been cleaned, but forensics have found tiny blood particles on them which match Zena Cattermole's."

"Good work, the pair of you," praised Livermore. "We're now getting a clearer picture of our killer. What can you tell us, Chris?"

Dimbleby rose to his feet with a smirk on his face. "I've been talking to Hobbs' doctor, and some equally interesting facts have emerged."

"Do enlighten us," Livermore encouraged.

"Well, my theory that the killer was either in prison or hospitalised during the four months between the last two murders proved to be correct. Hobbs went into hospital in July for an operation relating to his diabetes and liver problems, which he'd aggravated with drug abuse. So that would've kept him out of action for some weeks. His doctor also came up with another significant piece of information. It turns out that Hobbs was firing blanks."

"You mean he was impotent."

"Not exactly, Gov. He could get it up but not always for long enough to have intercourse. His doctor, a lady by the rather appropriate name of Miss Cox, told me he'd been going to her for treatment for some time for both a physical and psychological problem."

Dimbleby referred to his notebook before adding, "Hobbs suffered from retrograde ejaculation, which prevented him producing any semen. Apparently, RE is a condition in which part or all of a man's semen goes into the bladder instead of out of the tip of the penis during ejaculation."

"Ah," exclaimed Nottage, "that explains why we didn't find any on the three murder victims."

"It must've screwed him up that he couldn't screw properly," gloated Dimbleby, laughing at his own feeble joke. "He must have hated women."

Livermore cracked his knuckles and paused for effect before correcting him. "I should imagine that Hobbs desired women but felt uncomfortable in engaging in any sort of intercourse with them – either sexual or social."

Nottage nodded and then reflected with a wry smile, "It's so ironic Hobbs didn't seem to be aware that Zena Cattermole was a nightclub dancer who gave sexual favours for cash. In her job she presumably entertained some real creeps, but Hobbs must've been so obnoxious or threatening that she ran out on him."

"Yes," agreed Livermore. "Perhaps he also made a mistake in thinking that Zena had some sort of relationship with his brother. Justin hadn't actually gone out with her – they'd only met at a social evening. So Hobbs' decision to turn up at her flat, posing as Justin, might've been a surprise to her. He blagged his way in but then gave her cause for alarm.

"It would appear Hobbs simply didn't know how to behave in women's company. Maybe that partly explains why he developed abnormal sexual tastes, but it must stem from him being abused by his step-parents. He became so twisted that he derived pleasure from inflicting pain on women."

O'Sullivan chipped in, "No doubt sticking his metal sheath up their backsides compensated for his inadequacies and gave him power over them."

Livermore pondered this. "You're probably right. And his craving for power was no doubt heightened by the intense jealously he built up against Justin. The fact that the women he preyed upon preferred his brother must've been too much for him to accept."

"Ah, I can sympathise with him there," chimed in Dimbleby. "My bloody brother once. . ."

Livermore cut him short by holding up his hand.

"Sorry, Gov," mumbled the red-faced detective sergeant. "One thing I don't understand is why Hobbs picked on Zena Cattermole and Katrina Merton. They weren't in the dating agency brochure he nicked from Justin's flat. And he didn't know them, did he?"

Livermore took the trouble to explain. "Presumably he either didn't fancy the remaining women pictured in the brochure or couldn't track them down. It seems he contacted the agency, again posing as Justin, to get details of more recent female members, which included Zena and Katrina. He liked what he saw and decided to pay them a visit. For all we know, he may have been stalking his brother and seen him with Katrina. Now has anyone got anything else to contribute?"

Dimbleby suddenly broke wind. The sound was most unpleasant but the smell even worse. "Sorry," he mumbled. "I told my wife it was a mistake to give me those baked beans for breakfast."

His colleagues erupted with laughter.

O'Sullivan wiped away a tear from his eye as he blurted out, "Nice one, Chris. That was probably your best contribution yet. On a more serious note, I reckon Hobbs had a bloodlust that could never be satisfied. He'd probably have knifed his victims even if they'd consented to sex with him."

"That's debatable, but we'll never know," said Livermore. "Thank goodness Katrina Merton outwitted him."

"Yes," reflected Nottage. "She could easily have been his fourth victim. Instead, she killed him with what ballistics may find to be the same gun that was used to murder Hugo Protheroe in the college car park. It's certainly very similar. When she's eventually fit enough to be interviewed, she has some explaining to do."

CHAPTER SIXTY-NINE

Wednesday, 23 October 2013

Katrina had been recovering in her mother's bungalow in Newhaven and was sitting in the ornament-filled lounge doing a crossword when Livermore visited her.

He had explained on the telephone that he wanted to see how she was recovering, but Katrina was full of dread as he declined her offer of tea and seated himself opposite her.

"I suggested to my mother that she went shopping so that we could be alone," she told him.

"Very wise. Now how are you, Katrina? Still feeling traumatised?"

Crossing her legs and composing herself, she replied, "It was an awful experience I'll never forget, but my biggest concern now is finding out what's going to happen to me."

"When the doctor says you're fit enough, you can come into Sussex House to be interviewed."

"Look, Chief Inspector, I'm worried out of my mind. I need to be told the worst now."

"Well, you've become something of a vigilante, haven't you?"

"Not intentionally."

"I fully accept that it was self-defence when you killed Victor Remington – sorry, let's call him by his real name of Victor Hobbs. But you did so with the same gun that was used to shoot Hugo Protheroe. You'll recall that I agreed I wouldn't investigate further why your fingerprints were in the car in which Protheroe was found unless more evidence came to light or you were linked with a second killing. Both things have now occurred."

Katrina's attempt to put on a brave front was not working. Suddenly her nerve failed, and she could not prevent her eyes welling up with tears.

"All right, Chief Inspector. There's no need to taunt me about it. Just charge me with two killings."

Livermore looked at her for a full minute before replying. "These things are ultimately decided by the Crown Prosecution Service, but I will be recommending to them that you are not charged in relation to shooting Victor Hobbs. I'm confident they will accept it was self-defence."

"Thank you. So there's just the small matter of me killing Protheroe. Can we get it over with, please?"

"Let me ask you, Katrina: What assurance can you give me that you'd never do anything like that again?"

"Of course, I wouldn't. I'm wracked with guilt and will probably suffer nightmares about these killings for the rest of my life. I can't tell you how many sleepless nights I've had since the car park episode. I was terrified Protheroe would attack my sister again like he threatened to do, so I felt I had to frighten him off. I certainly didn't intend to kill him. But I realise that your hands are tied and I have to be charged. You've no option, have you?"

"Actually, I have," he said with the trace of a smile.

"Sorry?" she asked disbelievingly. "What do you mean?"

"The fingerprints you provided for elimination purposes when your mother was robbed have now been destroyed in accordance with police procedures. Only I know for sure that they match those in the Rover – I simply followed up a hunch that either you or your sister might've been in the car with Protheroe, seeing that you regularly used the same car park and your sister had been assaulted there.

"As you kept your word in helping me find the killer of three women, I'm going to take a charitable view on your part in all this."

"You mean I'll get off with manslaughter?"

"The fact that Protheroe had a knife with him in the car suggests his killer was again acting in self-defence. If it went to court, I don't think any jury would find you guilty of murder and probably not even manslaughter.

"Protheroe had assaulted and terrorised several women and came close to killing one of them when she put up a fight, so we're well shot of him, if you'll pardon the pun. In the circumstances, I'm going to make a recommendation that should ensure no charges will be brought against you, Katrina."

301

"But what about the gun?"

"Ah, yes, the gun. Well, that would normally be conclusive proof of your guilt, especially as you could have obtained it from your contacts with the Intelligence Corps or from your late father who belonged to a pistol club before all handguns were outlawed in 1997. Add that to the fact you had the motive of wanting to avenge the attack on your sister and you could be in deep shit."

Katrina's heart pounded – she was still expecting the worst.

But Livermore smiled. "It was fortunate that you phoned me on the special number I gave you immediately after you'd shot Hobbs. It meant I arrived at the crime scene first and 'checked' the evidence before you phoned the station to summon my colleagues.

"You told me you'd worn plastic disposable gloves when you loaded the revolver to avoid your prints being on the bullets. That was very wise of you. But there would've been forensic traces of gun oil and power residue on the cloth in which you'd wrapped the gun inside your shoebox. Luckily for you, there's no sign now of either the cloth or the box. And the mobile on which you phoned me has disappeared as well."

"Good grief! You disposed of them."

"I can't possibly comment on such a suggestion, Katrina. What I can tell you is that traces of gun oil were found in the pocket of Hobbs' coat, and his DNA is on the gun."

"So that's what you were doing when you were bending over his body . . . You must have placed the gun inside his pocket and then pressed his fingers against the handle."

"Those are dreadful accusations to make against a police officer, Katrina, and you must never repeat them. All you need to know is that the indications are the gun belonged to Hobbs. I trust you took my advice and said nothing."

"I didn't breathe a word to anyone. I was in such shock I could hardly speak anyway."

"Excellent. My report will highlight that Victor Hobbs used to be a member of a shooting club and had a love of guns as well as knives. Furthermore, he was booted out of the armed forces for his Rambo tendencies. So it would be reasonable to assume that he went to your flat armed with both knife and gun. My conclusion will be that the gun you used to shoot Hobbs was brought into your flat by him."

"But, if he's supposed to own the gun, how can you explain that it was used to kill Protheroe?"

"Good question. I'm sure that's the very point my detective inspector Nottage will raise when the ballistics report comes through. Nottage suspects you shot Protheroe and that it was you who tampered with the evidence in your flat by putting Hobbs' prints on the gun after you had shot him as well.

"But I'll be telling him – and the CPS – there's a simple answer, which is that Hobbs and Protheroe must have known each other. They fell out, and that resulted in Protheroe being shot by Hobbs."

"Is it possible their paths could have crossed?"

"It is, actually. They were both members of Eastbourne Library and had an interest in the same type of books, so they could have met there. Maybe Hobbs discovered Protheroe was a rapist and thought he should follow in his footsteps – even take over from him. I'll conclude that they quarrelled while in the Rover in the college car park, Protheroe pulled a knife, and Hobbs shot him. That should mean both cases will be closed."

Katrina was dumbfounded. "You're such a lovely man to do this for me," she eventually gasped, putting her hand to her mouth by way of both relief and surprise. "I can't thank you enough. But does it all make sense? How would Protheroe have got into the Rover? And why would Remington – sorry, Hobbs – have been in the car with him?"

Livermore shrugged. "It's easy to break into a car, especially one that old on which the alarm no longer worked. As for Hobbs, he might've wanted to help Protheroe commit a rape."

"And how will your report explain that Hobbs foolishly gave me the gun with which to shoot him?"

The chief inspector smiled again. "The teeth marks on part of his anatomy prompt me to assume that you defused his little weapon in order to get your hands on his big weapon, one of which he'd been brandishing about. Or have I got the sizes the wrong way around?"

They laughed together at his joke.

"When you told me about the treble tease of teeth, thighs, and tits, I thought you meant showing your teeth by smiling – not sinking them into the most sensitive part of a man's body." Again they laughed.

"If I hadn't already decided otherwise, I'd say you were guilty of performing a TRIPLE triple tease – first on Protheroe, then Justin, and finally Victor. But, of course, I've ruled you out of the Protheroe murder.

"So all I have to do now is to carry out a formal video-recorded interview with you under caution, in which you claim that Victor brought both the gun and the knife into your flat to threaten you. When that's submitted to the CPS, together with my recommendations, you should have nothing to worry about. But, as you will already have been informed, you can have a solicitor present at the interview if you wish."

"Perhaps I'll bring Boris Kimble along, but I know what to say – and what to leave out."

"Good. As long as you exercise your right to decline giving any fingerprints, you cannot be connected to the shooting of Protheroe. Hobbs can take the rap for that."

She got up, walked over to him, and planted a big kiss on his cheek.

"I trust this experience has put the fear of God into you, Miss Merton, so that you'll never handle a gun again."

*****

Livermore experienced the fear of God himself that evening when he got home to hear his wife boom at him. "Have you been with another woman, Harvey? What the devil's that red lipstick doing on your face?"

EPILOGUE

The revelation that the serial killer was an identical triplet who had met his own death at the hands of his intended fourth victim brought massive media coverage.

Katrina was hailed as a heroine for managing to grab hold of Victor Hobbs' gun and shoot him before he could stab her. Livermore referred to "her commendable calmness and bravery in overcoming a ruthless killer".

Most of the media accepted the difficulties the police had faced, particularly as not even Justin and Monty Remington were aware they had a brother – let alone an identical one.

Not surprisingly, Ross Yardley was a notable exception. He labelled Livermore a modern-day Inspector Clouseau who had twice blundered by arresting the wrong triplet and refusing to believe Justin's truthful account that any of his DNA found on the victims had resulted from him meeting them prior to the murders.

"How could the police get it so wrong?" the scathing journalist taunted. "Yes, it can be hard to tell identical triplets apart, but, whereas Justin and Monty were both well groomed and healthy, Victor was a messed-up drug addict. So how did the boys in blue think strands of Victor's hair belonged to his brothers?"

Yardley was rewarded for his acerbic conclusions by being given a job as a columnist, but his ego and male chauvinism proved to be his undoing.

In his attempt at humour in his first column, he pointed out, "The killer's three strands of dark brown hair were among over a hundred hairs belonging to his last victim that were found on her dress. That is because the average woman loses between 50 and 100 strands each day. So when you see stray hairs in the shower, don't worry your pretty little heads about them, ladies. And if you should go bald, there's plenty of wigs to choose from."

The newspaper proprietor's alopecia-suffering daughter was among those offended – and Yardley was promptly sacked.

Interest switched to Katrina when the tabloids discovered her ongoing relationship with Justin. The fact that a former murder suspect was dating the glamorous woman who had killed one of his brothers, albeit in self-defence, produced a media frenzy. The headlines ranged from 'The odd couple' to 'The weirdest romance ever?', but Katrina and Justin rode it out.

The CPS accepted Livermore's findings, and a press release was issued praising his "brilliant detective work" in discovering that 'lady killer' Hobbs had also murdered Hugo Protheroe.

"Seems you've swapped roles," chided Buster when they met up for a drink. "You've graduated from being a bumbling Clouseau to super sleuth Sherlock Holmes."

"But I've forsaken my principles and broken the rules. That doesn't sit well with me."

"You did it for the greater good, Harvey. In my book, you deserve the public's respect and admiration."

"Try telling that to my wife, Buster. It's bloody amazing, isn't it? Almost everyone I've come across in this case is into rampant sex – yet me, the only poor sod who's not getting any, is accused by his wife of having an affair."

ightning Source UK Ltd.
ton Keynes UK
V04f0745250216

0UK00002B/66/P